KNIFE
IN THE
DARK

HAUNTED COLLECTION SERIES BOOK 6

Written by Ron Ripley
Edited by Emma Salam

ISBN: 979-8-89476-022-3
Copyright © 2018 by ScareStreet.com

ENTER THE REALM OF TERROR...

We'd like to take a moment to thank you for your support and invite you to join our VIP newsletter.

Dive deeper into the darkness with exclusive offers, early access to new releases, and bone-chilling deals when you sign up at www.ScareStreet.com.

Let the nightmares begin...

See you in the shadows,
Scare Street

CHAPTER 1

A LITTLE BIT OF HELP

Charlie Flynn loved the internet.

The world shopped online, and the packages were delivered at all hours of the day. They were left in front of houses, on the stoops of buildings, and on their foyers. People had everything from dental floss to movies shipped to them, and Charlie knew how to move it all.

There was a Romanian family that owned a string of gas stations, and they would sell DVDs and Blu-Rays. A nice, retired schoolteacher could move whatever watches and jewelry Charlie brought her.

Yes, Charlie thought, *the internet has made my world a better place.*

Snickering, he ducked through the back door of a new apartment building off Elm Street. A month earlier, he had watched a drunk man punch in the security code while saying the numbers out loud. From the back, it was only a short walk past the communal, coin-operated laundry machines, up half a flight of stairs, and into the front lobby.

The building's super was lazy, and from what Charlie had observed, the man spent most of his days sealed up in his office. Any package delivered to the residents was left piled in the lobby, beneath the mailboxes.

Charlie never took more than two; never from the same unit, and he made it a point to only visit the building once a week.

It was a routine he kept up throughout the city and one that paid well. Between his welfare checks and the money for the goods, Charlie was feeling good about life. He had a good amount of cash stashed away in his studio apartment, beneath a loose floorboard under his mattress.

Grinning, Charlie climbed the stairs into the lobby and took a look at the mailboxes.

His shoulders slumped when he saw there was only one package. A large, padded envelope slightly too big to fit into the narrow confines of the designated mailbox.

Charlie didn't hesitate, striding across the tiled floor and bending down to scoop up the parcel. As he turned on his heel and retraced his steps, he opened his messenger bag and dropped the envelope in.

By the time he reached the backdoor, Charlie's mood had improved. Even if the package didn't turn out to have anything valuable in it, he would have money in his account from the State, and there was plenty of cash at home.

Reflecting on his abundance of wealth, Charlie decided to make a quick stop at the package store on the corner of Elm and Middle. When he reached the store, Charlie spent only a few minutes browsing the shelves. He did it more to antagonize Henri, the owner, than anything else. The Haitian always kept a careful eye on Charlie, and Charlie knew why.

Henri suspected Charlie of theft.

He had, of course, but not the little nips the Haitian kept by the register. Charlie often lifted entire bottles of vodka, but that, like everything else in Charlie's world, was primarily for resale.

His own particular taste ran to rum. Bacardi's when he could get it. The Admiral's when he couldn't.

Tonight, Charlie told himself, *it's Bacardi.*

He focused on the rum, found a bottle of Bacardi, and brought it to the counter.

Henri's eyes never left Charlie's during the entire transaction, the Haitian's fingers flying over the keys of the register. Charlie paid in cash, dropped a couple of pennies into the 'Take a Penny, Leave a Penny' dish, and collected his bagged adult beverage.

He gave an exaggerated nod to Henri and left the store.

By the time he reached his apartment, Charlie was whistling a tune he had heard earlier in the supermarket but couldn't quite place. He was still whistling when he let himself into his home, tossed his keys on the counter, and made himself a drink before cooking up the beef flavored cup-o-noodles that would be his dinner.

Charlie carried the food to his bed, sank down on the worn mattress, and pushed his blanket aside. He powered up his laptop and accessed his digital copy of *Star Wars*. With the familiar sounds of the movie in the background, Charlie quickly ate his food and washed it down with the rest of the rum.

A pleasant, drunken buzz overtook him, and the apartment swam in his vision as he picked his messenger bag up and removed the package he had stolen. He opened it with an easy, well-practiced motion. He then, fished out the contents which consisted of a receipt and a bubble wrapped item.

A single printed page described the object as lot number 4412, NORUNIV67, and said the purchase price was $318.67.

Charlie grinned, dropped the paper, and unwrapped the item.

The object was a class ring, the name of the school worn but still legible.

Norwich University, Class of 1967.

Charlie turned the ring around in his hand and peered inside the band. He found an engraving that stated it had once belonged to Richard H. Bronte, and a stamp declaring the metal to be silver.

Looking at the stone set in the ring, Charlie realized it was semiprecious. A black, multi-faceted stone.

Onyx, he thought. *Don't know how much it's worth, but I can move the silver at least.*

He slid the ring onto his index finger, but the ring was far too large.

Damn, Charlie chuckled, *the guy must have been a giant.*

The metal, he noticed, was disturbingly cold, no matter how long he held it.

Frowning, Charlie set the ring down on the bed beside him, took a pleased sip of his drink, and tried to follow the story playing out on the computer.

Just as he seemed to finally get his thoughts together, the laptop's screen flickered, dimmed, and then went out. The light over the sink did the same, and in a heartbeat, only the light of the late afternoon illuminated the apartment.

Confused, Charlie straightened up and looked around bleary-eyed. He listened for the sound of emergency vehicles, wondering if perhaps someone had struck a telephone pole and knocked out the power to the neighborhood.

It had happened before and would happen again.

The room darkened and became chilly.

Shivering, Charlie reached out, found his blanket, and pulled it up around him.

"Who are you?" a voice hissed.

Panic welled up within Charlie, his throat tightening and refusing to allow him to speak.

"I asked you a question!" As the words filled the room, the shadows gathered together by the far wall, knitting themselves into the shape and form of a man.

Charlie shuddered once, felt his eyes roll up into his head, and fell backward onto his mattress, his head bouncing off the wall.

CHAPTER 2

IRRITATION

Oliver James Prescott IV arrived at his apartment building's parking garage, made certain his Audi A4 was locked and the security system armed, and then hurried through the sky-bridge that connected the garage to the building. Instead of taking the stairs up to the fifth floor and his home, Oliver descended them, making his way to the postal boxes in the main foyer. He had received an email stating the package he had ordered had arrived, and it had been signed for by the super.

Oliver collected class rings. Specifically, class rings from Norwich University, from which he, his father, and his paternal grandfather had graduated. Oliver often scoured the various sale sites on the internet, seeking Norwich rings and bringing them back into the fold, so to speak.

When he reached the postal boxes, Oliver glanced at the floor, where the super usually had the mailman leave the packages and sighed with relief. There was nothing to be seen, which meant the seller had sent the ring in an envelope small enough to fit into the building's miniscule mailboxes. A tremor of excitement rippled through him as he unlocked the box and opened it.

The excitement soured and turned to anger as Oliver removed a trio of utility bills and a single flyer for a new pizza shop one block up. Clenching them in a fist, he slammed the door closed, locked it, and stalked over to the super's door, which was, per usual, shut.

Oliver rang the cheap, wireless doorbell and counted to thirty before he pressed it again. He counted down from twenty and rang it once more. Oliver then repeated it at ten, five, and then back to ten. By the time he had cycled through his routine twice, he heard the angry shouts of the super.

Locks rattled, and the door opened.

The super squinted at him, lines exploding around his brown eyes, his pale skin mimicking the paper of the mystery books the man was always reading. He wore a tattered, faded red, terry-cloth robe, threadbare blue pajamas, and a pair of dull gray slippers that Oliver could see the man's socks through. In one of his thin, heavily veined hands the man held a large book, the author of which, Oliver noticed, was Agatha Christie.

"You keep ringing that bell," the super grumbled, "and I'll rip it off the God-damned wall. Then how will you get in touch with me?"

"I'll knock," Oliver snapped. "Where's my package?"

The super looked around at the mailboxes, then shrugged. "How the hell should I know?"

"You signed for it!" Oliver exclaimed.

"I sign for a lot," the super said, a bored tone in his voice. "Then I leave it out there so the residents can pick it up."

"You should have kept it in your apartment!" Oliver's voice almost reached a shriek of outrage as he spoke.

The other man shook his head. "Nope. Not in the contract. Read it sometime. Although, I'm pretty sure we've had this conversation before, Mr. Prescott. I'll sign for items if you want. After that, they go in front of the mailboxes. Don't like it, have 'em delivered somewhere else."

Before Oliver could argue the point any longer, the super stepped back and slammed the door in his face. The action was followed swiftly by the sound of the locks going back into place.

Shaking with rage, Oliver walked up the stairs, attempting to compose himself before reaching his apartment. By the time he arrived at the fourth floor, his anger had subsided to a thick, gelatinous sludge in his mind. It moved slowly within him, settling in as he considered how best to recoup his financial loss in regards to the ring. He also began to mentally compose a letter he was going to send to the management about the installation of a camera in the foyer.

Oliver wasn't the first to suffer a theft in the building, but he was going to be the last.

Arriving at his door, Oliver let himself in and walked straight to his desk. The door clicked shut behind him, and he sat down. He turned on his tower and the monitor, and in a matter of moments, he was logged onto eBay. Scrolling through his purchases, Oliver found the seller from whom he had bought the ring.

Keeping a lid on his anger, Oliver quickly created a new message and typed in a short statement.

Dear Haunted49Alpha,

The item which I purchased from you, a Norwich class ring from 1967, has vanished from my lobby due to the excessive packaging in which you placed the item. Since the container was too large to fit in my mailbox, it was stolen. I hold you responsible for the theft, and I am seeking a complete refund—including the price of shipping—from you. I shall give you 48 hours to respond to this request, and should I not hear from you, I will upgrade this to a formal complaint and file it with eBay.

Sincerely,
Oliver James Prescott IV

Oliver read over his letter several times, made a few minor corrections, and then clicked send.

With that finished, he opened up a new Word document and began to write an equally aggressive letter to the management.

Oliver would have his security and his money. Of that, he was certain.

CHAPTER 3

A NECESSARY BIT OF READING

Victor Daniels stood up, stretched, and rubbed his eyes. He had drifted off in his chair again, his mouth dry, and neck sore from the awkward position in which he had slept. Wincing, he stepped around his desk and out into the hall. He picked his way carefully to the kitchen and found Tom and Iris at the table.

"Morning or afternoon?" Victor asked, grinning at the two teens.

"Morning," Iris answered.

"Of Wednesday," Tom added.

Victor sighed. "Slept through the better part of Tuesday, I take it?"

Tom nodded as he adjusted a strap on his prosthetic. "A package came for you earlier. Pretty thick, too. It's from Moran and Moran."

The name of the sender drove the last vestiges of sleep from Victor; the knowledge of what the company specialized in helped sweep aside the cobwebs clinging to his thoughts.

"Is it in the study?" Victor asked.

"Yes," Tom said. "There's fresh coffee, too, if you want to take a cup with you."

Victor smiled and nodded his thanks. When he had his mug filled, Victor carried it with him to the study. On the desk lay a large, manila envelope. The address and return address were written in the elegant script he could attribute to James Moran III. Sitting down, Victor took a cautious sip of his drink and set it on the table.

The envelope opened easily, and Victor withdrew a large sheaf of printed pages, the topmost of which was of a thicker weight, and a soft ivory instead of the harsh white of the others.

The letterhead was that of Moran and Moran, and like the address on the envelope, the note was written in James' perfect handwriting.

My Dear Mr. Daniels,

Here is the information which you requested from us. This is a detailed list of each item which was sold to either Nicole or Ivan Denisovich Korzh through our establishment. At the end, I have appended a list of items which I suspect were purchased by Ivan Denisovich over the years at other auctions, or through private sales. It is, as I am sure you can tell, a large amount.

In addition to the descriptions of the individual pieces, I have jotted down what little I know of them. For example, you will find mention of a single piece of curved, light green sea glass. It is, as far as we know, the sole surviving piece of a shipwreck off the coast of New Jersey in the early 1900s. There is a young sailor attached to it, yet he is, from what we know, a benign entity.

I hope this information is useful to you, and that it will help you bring some sort of resolution in regards to Stefan Korzh.

Your friend,
James P. Moran III

Victor set James' note aside and looked at the stack of paper. He suspected there were at least a hundred pages, if not more. Settling back into his chair, Victor picked up the first page and began to read.

He needed to know what might be out there and to think of a way to find them.

If he couldn't stop Korzh, Victor could at least find the items the killer was intent on spreading throughout the country.

CHAPTER 4

A DARK DREAM

Richard hovered in the background, close to Charlie and the ring as they entered the bar. A thrill went through him as he looked at the people gathered within, and he wondered who among them was drunk enough to be controlled.

So drunk that I might have myself a little bit of fun, Richard thought, smiling.

His eyes fell upon an older woman at the end of the bar, a glass of wine clutched in her hand. Richard could sense her weakness from across the room and he shivered with anticipation.

He imagined the pleasure of possession, and he remembered the thrill of a body under his command.

Richard recalled his last night of life, when he had come so close to dining on the delicate flesh of a young Indian girl. He had acquired a taste for human meat in the jungles of Southeast Asia, and even in death, his longing for it had not diminished.

Once he had control of the woman at the end of the bar, he would be able to find a bite to eat.

Richard shuddered, and he realized that if he had a mouth with which to salivate, he would have.

Quivering with pleasure, he glided toward her.

***

Gwen sat at the bar, holding onto her glass of pinot noir with the same strength she held onto the edge of her seat. She had finished off at least one bottle in celebration of her thirty-fifth birthday, was well into her second, and she was feeling exceptionally amorous. Her expectations had been high, as always, when she had entered the pub sober.

More drunk than she wanted to be, her standards had lowered significantly.

When the door to the pub opened and the young man walked in, she almost didn't notice him.

But it was as if someone was beside her, whispering in her ear, encouraging to look at the stranger with fresh eyes.

Gwen did so, and she had a sudden appreciation for the young man's rakish appearance. For some reason, the large class ring on his index finger caught her eye and held her attention.

Standing up, she walked with far more grace and ease than she thought herself capable of after so much wine, and stopped beside him. She smiled, reached her hand out, and introduced herself.

***

Charlie had barely made it out of his apartment after the horrific incident with the creature in the ring.

He shuddered at the memory of the mad scramble to get out of his apartment, to get away from the creature lurking in the darkness. Part of him couldn't believe it.

Don't believe it, he snapped at himself. But before he could continue with his self-reproach, a hand on his arm interrupted him.

He managed not to jerk away as he looked at the person beside him.

For a heartbeat, he couldn't find his voice.

An attractive, older woman smiled up at him. Her lips were full and covered expertly with deep red lipstick. The woman's eyes, which were a stunning green, focused on him hungrily, and she gave him a wink.

"I'm Gwen," she said, offering her hand.

"Charlie," he answered, shaking it.

"That's a good name," she replied. She finished the last of her wine, set the empty glass on the bar and asked, "Do you want to get out of here, Charlie?"

He almost stated that he had just arrived, and he wasn't drunk, but he managed to stop himself.

"Yeah," he replied, nodding, "getting out of here would be a great idea. Where do you want to go?"

She nodded towards the side exit, leaned in close and whispered just above the steady murmur of the other patrons, "The alley's a good place to start."

Charlie's heart thundered in his chest and he nodded, his mouth suddenly dry with anticipation. She took his hand and let him lead the way to the exit.

Charlie did so happily, and after weaving his way past other couples, he and Gwen reached the door. He pushed it open and stepped out into the cool evening air. As the door thunked closed behind them, Charlie turned to speak with her.

But the words died in his mouth as something struck him in the center of his forehead.

**

Gwen opened her eyes, rolled over and vomited.

Bile spewed out of her mouth and burned her nostrils. She gagged, threw up again, and wiped her mouth with the back of her hand.

Drawing in great, shuddering breaths, Gwen groaned as she thought about the mess that she had to clean. She looked down and froze.

Instead of her bed, Gwen was looking down at asphalt, dimly lit by an orange streetlamp at the end of a small alley.

Frantic, Gwen pushed herself against a wall and looked around.

Trash and debris littered the cracked and broken ground of the alley. Battered brick walls flanked either side and there were no windows until the second floor. Rusted fire escapes were suspended above her, and graffiti-covered steel doors were closed and secured.

And beside Gwen was a body.

A strangled scream escaped her throat as she scrambled backward, slamming her head into the brick behind her.

Gasping for air, Gwen stared at the corpse, and she had no doubt the man was dead.

He lay on his back, throat cut so deeply that his head hung by a thread of skin. Blood covered the man's once-white shirt and soaked the front of his black pants. Battered black Nike sneakers were also damp, their dirty soles surprisingly free of his blood. His arms were spread wide as if he was awaiting crucifixion. Dark brown hair stuck to his head in damp clumps and was spread out with the vile semblance of a blood-soaked halo.

Beside the body was a knife. It was a folding knife; black and stamped with the letters SOG.

Oh no, she thought, her inner voice building up to a panic. *Oh no, no, no, no!*

She lifted her hands up to clutch her head, but stopped, horrified when she saw she was covered in blood as well.

For a moment, she froze, mind completely incapable of understanding what she saw, and then a shudder tore through her.

She scrambled forward, snatched the knife up from the ground, and wiped the blade off on the man's pants. Closing the weapon, Gwen got to her feet, eyes darting around the narrow confines of the alley.

She tore off her jacket, wiped her hands on it until most of the blood was gone, then turned it inside out. Shuddering, she pulled the jacket back on, her skin crawling as the sticky, cool blood touched her. She stuffed her hands into her front pockets, licked her lips nervously, and then hurried down the alley to the street beyond.

A glance to the left showed she was on Singleton Street. Three blocks from home if she followed the sidewalk.

Gwen didn't.

Instead, she forced herself to walk casually to the next alley and turned towards it. Grinding her teeth, Gwen continued at her steady, mild pace, the minutes ticking past.

When she reached her building, Gwen climbed the stairs two at a time, got into her apartment, and sank against the door when she closed it. Sobbing, she drew her hands out of her pockets, and for the first time, she noticed she was wearing a large class ring on her right index finger.

She went to take it off, but her skin was swollen, the jewelry stuck. Her mother would know how to get the ring off. Gwen couldn't ask her though. They hadn't spoken in years, and she knew she couldn't call about the ring.

Mom would want to know why, she thought. *Where the ring came from. Am I in trouble, again.*

Gwen let out a short laugh, but it came out so maniacally that she clamped her hand over her mouth.

Shower. Take a shower, she told herself, getting up to her feet and swaying dizzily. Stripping off her blood-stained clothes, Gwen made it into the shower and scrubbed herself clean beneath a sputtering spray of near-boiling hot water.

She dried off hastily, wrapped the towel around her chest, and walked numbly to her small kitchen. From the counter, she reached for a bottle of wine, removed the cork, and took a long, bitter swallow. The alcohol rushed through her system, and she quickly took several deep drinks.

With her mouth stinging from the wine, Gwen left the bottle on the counter and stumbled to her bed, where she collapsed. She stared up at the cracked ceiling, the paint-stained a dull yellow from the previous tenant's nicotine habit.

Goosebumps rippled along her flesh and Gwen shivered, pulling her blanket up over her.

She tried to think, sought to remember what had happened and why she had been in the alley. But nothing came to her.

The last memory she had was of approaching someone in the pub.

"Tell me, Gwen," a soft voice said, "did you enjoy it?"

Gwen froze, unable to move. She recognized the voice. It was the same one she had heard when she had been drinking at the pub.

"I know you can hear me," the stranger said, and movement on the far wall demanded Gwen's attention.

Unable to look away, she watched as the shadow across from her solidified and took on definition.

A young man, perhaps only a decade younger than herself, stood before her. The man wore olive-drab fatigues and black combat boots. His sleeves were rolled up to reveal well-defined forearms, and there was a sinister strength that exuded from the stranger.

"Who are you?" Gwen's words came out in a hoarse, desperate whisper.

"You don't remember our earlier conversation?" the young man asked. When Gwen didn't respond, the stranger sighed. "Very well. You're wearing my ring, you foul little drunk. My name is Richard."

Gwen's eyes flicked down to the ring on her hand, and she resisted the urge to cut her own finger off.

"What happened?" Gwen asked. "Why was that man dead?"

"I happened," Richard smirked, settling down on his haunches. "And he's dead because I wanted him to be dead. He was annoying. And a thief. And all thieves should be dead. Don't you agree?"

"No," Gwen answered, horrified. "No!"

"That's a shame, Gwen." Richard smiled. "Because as long as we're together, you're going to help me make a lot of people dead."

Gwen tried to wrench the ring off her finger, but as her hand wrapped around it, she found Richard upon her.

CHAPTER 5

IN DEEP DARKNESS

Leanne Le Monde ascended the stairs with slow and measured steps. A weariness had settled into her bones, and a reluctance over what needed to be done weighed upon her. At the landing, she turned left and walked to the tall, narrow door set deep within an alcove.

The door was a dull gray, the grain of the wood forming curious swirls that, when looked upon for more than a heartbeat, twisted and shifted in a pattern that could dizzy and mesmerize. A crystal-cut knob extended from a stamped brass plate, and brass hinges held the door in the frame. Made from a single piece of wood, the door gave the impression that it led to nothing more significant than a linen closet, or perhaps housed a pull-down ironing board.

Leanne knew better, and so would anyone who recognized the wood. It had been culled from a yew tree, one raised and bred in the wilds of Wales. And the door opened on nothing as mundane as a linen closet.

From her waist, Leanne retrieved a small silver ring of keys, all of which were old and formed of steel. She selected the one she needed, the minute key with a round barrel and a trio of spikes that extended in a triangular fashion from it. Stepping forward, Leanne inserted the key, waited a moment until she heard a gentle click, then turned it slowly to the right until a second click sounded. Finally, she twisted the key sharply to the left and a loud hiss exhaled around the seams of the door, as if the frame released it.

Leanne withdrew the key, replaced the ring on her waist, and grasped the cool crystal knob in her ancient hand. Bracing herself, Leanne twisted the doorknob hard to the left, and pulled back.

The door hinges sighed, a mild rebuke for the decades they had remained unused. A hot-house warmth pulsed out of the door and delicate tendrils of smoke crept out from the darkness beyond.

Leanne paused at the threshold, hand still upon the crystal, allowing her eyes to adjust to the absence of light. They did so within a matter of heartbeats, and then she could see a narrow corridor in front of her.

It extended for exactly seventy-four steps, well past the boundaries of the house.

But the door didn't lead into any room in the house. Or to any room in the world in which she had resided for two centuries.

Leanne stepped over the threshold and into the hall, and out of her shoes. Her bare feet found the smooth cobblestones she recalled so well, and she rested a hand on the cool, dark wood that walled the corridor in. She closed the door behind her and began the trek in near darkness.

With every step she took, Leanne found her vision improving. Details leaped into view, the gentle curves of carved leaves running along the top of the wall, faces of wood nymphs peering out from the same.

Her steps became lighter, her legs stronger. She felt her back straighten, and her ears grew keener, the sounds of her steps loud, but not loud enough to mask the noises coming from the end of the hallway.

Leanne was nearly at a run when she reached the end of the corridor, reaching a door which was the twin to the one she had opened within her house.

There was no hesitation and no need for a key.

The door knew her and sprang open when she stopped before it.

Light burst out and wrapped around her. The smell of fresh meat and the pungent odor of flowers primed for spring rolled over her. Voices that had been raised in song and merriment went silent, and figures that had been dancing but a moment before stood frozen in surprise around a bonfire piled high with thick logs and thin bones.

The blaze crackled and snapped while a full moon shined down upon the scene before her.

Bound and chained human firstborns cowered at the sight of her. A pair of lycanthropes pushed themselves back into shadows, and a grim looking man with an eternally youthful face stood up from his seat on a raised dais.

A look of fear flashed across his cruel features, his long, pointed ears twitching. He reached up with a hand that trembled only slightly and brushed a lock of dark hair out of his face. His clothes were a deep black, and they rustled as he offered Leanne a deep bow.

When he straightened up, he had regained his composure, and there was no longer any trace of fear on his face.

"Dear Lady," he said in his rich baritone, "what brings you to us?"

"Vengeance," Leanne replied, her voice young once more.

Several of those around the fire shrank back, and she sneered at them.

"Not you, fools." She laughed and shook her head. "I have a task, one I cannot do alone. And there are many among you who are bound to me."

The man acknowledged the statement with a stiff nod of his head. "What would you have of us do, then?"

"Someone who still moves through the shadows," she said, her voice sinking. "One who still breeds nightmares and revels in them."

"She isn't here," the man replied. "We know not—"

Leanne snarled, and he shut his mouth.

"Have you forgotten who I am?" she asked. No one met her gaze. "I am the eldest of you all, and it was my daughter who sat upon that chair. My child murdered. You will not deny me, for if you do, I will wreak havoc on you as no other ever has."

The fear around the fire was palpable.

"Go," the man said, motioning to all around the fire, his voice trembling. "Find her. Bring her here. No matter the cost."

Lycanthropes darted away, and the shackled humans hobbled along after the shapeshifters.

Leanne walked around the fire and went up to the dais. The man bowed again and stepped aside. Leanne sat down, her youthful fingers tracing the screaming faces carved into the wooden arms.

Staring into the flames of the bonfire, Leanne listened to the nervous breathing of the man and waited for the dark one to be brought to her.

CHAPTER 6:
AN UNWANTED INTERRUPTION

When Stefan Korzh checked his email, his anger spiked.

A notification from his eBay account informed him of a complaint from a buyer with regards to a purchase. Gritting his teeth, Korzh logged into his profile and checked the message.

He read it over three times, not quite certain how the buyer, Oliver James Prescott IV, could hold him responsible for the theft of an item. The packaging had been perfect, as it always was because building a solid profile on the various selling platforms ensured a quicker dispersal of his parents' collection.

And the man wanted his money back.

You're not getting your money back, you idiot, Stefan thought angrily. As he wrote his response, he did not call the man an idiot, although he wanted to. In fact, he withheld from calling Mr. Prescott anything other than 'sir', which took some work.

> *Dear Sir,*
>
> *I am quite sorry to hear that you have suffered the theft of your recent purchase. Unfortunately, I cannot be held responsible for such a random act, nor can I be held accountable for the diminutive stature of your mailbox. I have sold a great many items, and not once have I received a complaint regarding packaging.*
>
> *Perhaps, sir, you should have stated the size of your mailbox when you won the bid. I wish you the best of luck in the retrieval of your stolen item.*

Stefan did not attach his name to the message, and he sent it off as soon as he finished.

Standing up, he left the room and went into his bedroom. He put his wallet in his pocket, holstered a small, .22 semi-automatic pistol, and picked up the keys for his truck. His heart fluttered for a moment as he adjusted his eye patch, and he clamped down on his fear.

He knew Anne Le Morte, and her newest caretaker was out and about. And he had not yet received all of the materials he had ordered for increased security. In addition to that, he had several more of his mother's haunted possessions he needed to ship out.

Stefan hesitated in his room and thought about his father.

Ivan Denisovich's private room, the one filled with the worst of the Korzh collection, was still under lock and key in the old home. And while Stefan was making headway in the dispersal of primarily his mother's collection, his vengeance wouldn't be complete until he managed to get into the room.

At times, such an act seemed impossible. Not only did Stefan not have the key, but his father was still haunting the room.

And don't forget Ariana, Stefan thought bitterly, leaving his room. *She's still out there, too.*

His anger flared up again, and he stuffed it down. He needed to focus, or else he risked another incursion into his warehouse.

Stefan shook his head at the memory of the initial fight with the hunter, and he understood that it had been little more than luck that had helped him win.

Vigilance and perseverance were needed, especially with Anne on the loose. And the unknown caretaker was a threat as well. Who knew what skills or abilities were brought to the situation by the individual.

Jingling his keys nervously, Stefan picked up the box of packaged items which needed to be shipped. He left the safety of his rooms and walked across through the interior of the warehouse to his pickup truck. Setting the box on the passenger seat, Stefan climbed in, started the engine, and headed towards the building's main exit.

***

Grace Whiting sat in the deep shadow of a large pine tree and stared at the pick-up truck as it passed through the gate to the parking lot. A man climbed out of the truck, his head turning from left to right and back again as he walked to the gate and closed it with the same speed with which he had opened it.

"Is that him?" she asked in halting French.

The cold, porcelain doll with the tattered, dirty white dress answered in the most beautiful voice Grace had ever heard.

"Yes," Anne Le Morte stated. "Will you help me kill him, dear one?"

"Of course," Grace answered. She watched the man get into the truck and speed off, the rocks and pebbles kicked back by the vehicle's tires clanged off the fence. "When?"

"Soon," Anne said. "Rest now."

Grace nodded and got to her feet, her knees sending threads of pain through her nerves. She stumbled for several steps, but her hold on the doll never loosened.

"Do you need to eat?" Anne asked, her voice filled with concern.

"Yes," Grace said, her stomach growling at the thought of food.

"There is a market, not far from here," Anne answered. "Follow the road, but do not walk upon it."

Grace nodded and began her trek. She didn't have any money. There was no need to bring any, not when she had gone climbing with Mark.

But stores had dumpsters, and Grace was certain she could find something to eat in one.

Chapter 7

Evidence and Conclusions

Victor's eyes were tired. He had spent the better part of the morning and early afternoon searching the internet for any mention of the items on the list James Moran had mailed to him.

Victor had found several, the most recent being the sale of a class ring on eBay. Each of them, according to the appendix, were attributed to murderers. Sitting in front of the computer, and rubbing at his eyes, Victor understood that he needed to search for deaths comparable to the modus operandi of the ghosts.

The idea of it was unpleasant. He had taken the 'safe search' parameters off Google, and he knew that there would be uncomfortable and disturbing images revealed for any search concerning killings.

Has to be done, he told himself, dropping his hands down. *So, I need to get it done.*

Victor leaned forward and typed in the first of the search terms.

For an hour, he poured over hideous photographs and crime scene documentation. None of which were related to the first three items.

The fourth, the class ring, triggered a response.

Bracing himself, Victor clicked on the article.

Man found with head nearly severed.

There was little more information than that, and there were no photographs. Victor hesitated only for a moment before he accessed the dark net and went searching for the images. He found them a few minutes later. A hacker in Belgium had posted them, bragging about hacking into Concord, New Hampshire police department's closed system.

The images were horrific, and Victor had to bite back his bile as he examined them. According to the information sent along by James Moran, there would be a distinct pattern in the stab wounds, in addition to near severing of the head.

Victor found the initial autopsy photographs and clicked on the first one, enlarging it.

The man's body had been washed clean, and the bloodless wounds gaped at the camera, drawing his eyes in.

> *Fifteen stab wounds, making an almost perfect circle from the sternum to the navel. Small incision in the left breast. 3 ounces of flesh missing.*

Victor read, and a glance at the appendix affirmed the statement.

Leaning back and away from the monitor, Victor shook his head, rubbed his face, and let out a sigh. Finally, he forced himself to look at the photograph again.

This, he told himself, *is why I'm not hunting Korzh through the Pennsylvania countryside right now. I need to put a stop to this ghost. He has to run out of items soon.*

But there was no conviction in the last statement.

Who knows how many possessed items Nicole and Ivan Denisovich Korzh had gathered over the years that aren't on any list or registry, Victor thought.

Don't think like that, he chided himself. *Focus. Look at him and remember.*

Once again, Victor looked at the dead man, then he closed the window and stood up. He went back to the kitchen to fix himself something to eat, and he found a note from Tom on the table.

> *Iris and I went to the mall. We should be back by dinner. Send me a text if you need anything.*

Victor smiled at the boy's thoughtfulness and put the note back on the table. He made himself a peanut butter sandwich, poured a glass of water, and sat down with it. Absently, Victor ate his lunch, and he had nearly finished when he felt a cold draft against his neck.

Did I leave a window open? he wondered. Standing up and popping the last bite of sandwich into his mouth, Victor nearly choked.

A ghost stood in the doorway to the hall, and the dead man was in horrific shape. It looked as though he had been gutted and shot repeatedly before he died, and that had made for an ugly and terrifying specter.

"You are Victor Daniels," the dead man said, grinning with a mouthful of broken teeth.

Victor cleared his throat, nodded and said, "I am. Who are you?"

"Bontoc will suffice," the ghost said, striding across the kitchen floor and sitting at the table. "It is my name, as for my surname, well, it is not important. Will you sit with me?"

Victor shook his head in disbelief, then, forcing the memories of what he had heard about the dead man away, he said, "Yes. Yes, I can do that."

Once he was seated, Victor looked at Bontoc and asked, "How did you get in my house?"

The dead man looked at him curiously for a moment, then he shrugged and said, "I am here with Tom."

Victor blinked and processed the information for a moment.

"Okay," Victor said, "want to run that by me again, please?"

Bontoc repeated himself, and Victor felt an angry heat rise up his neck and settle in his cheeks.

"Tom has a new ghost in his room?" Victor asked in a low voice. He wasn't sure what he was angrier about, the fact that there was a ghost he didn't know of in the boy's room, or that Tom had kept the information from him.

Victor took several deep breaths and forced himself to remember his own, private nature as a teen. With that memory rooted firmly in place, he found he could think clearly.

"I am sorry that he did not inform you," Bontoc said, and the dead man sounded genuinely sincere. "He is a good boy. I am certain that he meant no disrespect by it."

"You're right," Victor said. "I'm sure he didn't. Be that as it may, Bontoc, I would like to know what you are doing here. If it is not too forward of me, it looks as though you died... well... badly."

Bontoc smirked and nodded. "That would be correct. It was done by a mutual enemy of ours."

"Korzh," Victor said in a soft voice.

The dead man's face took on a mien of seriousness. "Yes. Stefan Korzh."

"Where did this happen?" Victor asked.

"Near his home, which," the ghost said, holding up a hand to forestall interruption, "is well-defended. Not only by Stefan but by Anne Le Morte as well."

"She's guarding it?" Victor asked, feeling a chill settle in the base of his spine.

"Not for him," Bontoc said, "but from any others claiming him. She has been tasked, as was I, with the death of Stefan Korzh. His father gave me the responsibility, and I still have a need to finish the job. Do you understand?"

Victor understood he hated Korzh, so he gave a short nod. "How do you plan on killing Korzh when you're dead, and for some reason you're stuck here, in my house?"

Bontoc gave him a grim smile.

"Unfortunately," the dead man said, "I am not quite certain as to how that will be accomplished. At least not yet. I merely made my presence known because I felt I should introduce myself, and to be quite honest, I had assumed Tom spoke with you."

"I would have made that assumption myself," Victor murmured.

The ghost stood up, hesitated, and asked, "Will you keep our conversation to yourself? I do not wish to upset our mutual friend."

Victor nodded, chuckled, and then said, "Yes. Yes, I will."

"Excellent," Bontoc said, giving him a short bow. "Many thanks, Victor Daniels. It was a pleasure to speak with you. I hope we might be able to do so again soon."

Victor watched the dead man leave, and he wondered how long it had taken the ghost to die, and how badly he had made Stefan Korzh suffer.

CHAPTER 8:
A PLEASANT, INFORMATIVE CONVERSATION

Gwen was wrapped in her blankets, the hood of her sweatshirt pulled up over her head. Her room was dark, but she knew Richard was in the apartment with her.

It was cold. Terribly cold. As if someone had trapped winter within the confines of the four walls and sealed the building to ensure none of the chill escaped.

"Tell me, Gwen," Richard said from the darkness. "How are you feeling?"

"Terrible," Gwen answered, her teeth chattering as she spoke. "What do you want from me?"

"We've gone over this," Richard said. His tone was patient, pleasant. "Do we really need to cover it again?"

"I'm not helping you kill anyone," Gwen hissed.

"Oh, but you already have." Richard chuckled. "I've been dead a long time, Gwen. Almost fifty years. I scratched my particular itch a few times in Vietnam. And several times on a few of the Indian reservations here in the States, but not nearly enough."

"It's not an itch," Gwen whispered. "You're a killer."

"Of course, I am," Richard replied. "Good Lord, Gwen, what do you think they taught me to do in the army? I was a lieutenant in an infantry unit. All we did was kill when we found them."

Richard paused, then stated, "You know, I think you might be a shade more attractive if we trim that long hair of yours."

"Don't touch my God damned hair!" Gwen shouted, suddenly furious.

"Ah, are you the proverbial Samson?" Richard asked.

"Who?" Gwen asked, confused.

She heard the dead man sigh. "Anyway, if we might get back to the subject at hand, as I was saying, you're going to help me kill. You don't have a choice."

"Of course, I do," Gwen snapped. "I'm not going to. In fact, I'm going to get good and drunk, and rip this ring off my finger."

Richard chuckled. "By all means, Gwen, be my guest. You won't want to, once you're drunk. And even if you get drunk enough, you won't be able to."

"I'll cut it off!" Gwen shook with fear and rage.

"Oh, I don't think so," Richard said in a cool, measured voice.

"Yeah? Why's that?" Gwen demanded.

"Because," the dead man said, "I'll stop you."

"You can't stop me," Gwen started, but her voice stopped short. A cold, steel grip wrapped around her throat and squeezed. It choked off her oxygen, and as she tried to claw at the unseen hand, she discovered there was nothing to remove. No fingers to grab. No arm to punch.

Nothing.

The grip vanished, and Gwen fell forward, half off the bed, gasping for breath and retching. After several minutes, she was able to push herself back into a sitting position.

"Why?" Gwen's question came out as a sob. "Why are you doing this to me?"

Richard let out a laugh. "Because I can. Why does anyone do anything, Gwen? Because we can. Not because it is right or it is wrong, but merely because I have the strength of will to do what it is I want. There is a pure and untainted joy to be found in being the master of your own fate. And I must ask, although I trust I already know the answer, do you have any idea of the thrill of watching another person die?"

Gwen couldn't answer the question. She couldn't even fathom a response.

"Hm," Richard murmured. "I suppose not. So few do. It's a pity, you know that people don't enjoy such acts. So many social ills could be solved with the cultivation of such taste. Criminals, vagabonds. How few of those would remain if we were allowed to sate our needs with them."

Gwen sank down onto her bed and pulled the blankets over her head.

"Have a drink, Gwen," the dead man said. "Relax. The night is young. Hell, we have so much time to look forward to. Are you looking forward to it?"

Gwen's response was a mournful sob.

CHAPTER 9:
BENEATH THE WORLD

Her ears twitched, and she looked up from the depths of the wine trapped in her decanter.

Leanne saw the female as she approached the dais, her fur a sleek dark brown tinged with silver. She strode forward on two legs, each paw sure and true. Her body was slim and youthful in appearance, but the silver around the muzzle and the maturity in the eyes told Leanne she was looking upon one of the hunters of the were-folk.

A female not to be trifled with.

Leanne smiled. She could appreciate that.

The female came to a stop, ten feet from the chair, and bowed low.

"To the elder," the creature said in a smooth, silken voice. "I bring myself to answer your summons."

"Your name?" Leanne asked.

"Inconsequential," the female replied, "but if you must have a title by which to call me, then Cane will suffice."

Leanne's lip twitched with pleasure, and she nodded.

"For what purpose do you require my services?" Cane asked.

"I seek out justice for a breathing man," Leanne replied, "and the taking and transplanting of a live one surpasses my abilities at this time."

"Would you have such a one brought to you?" Cane asked.

Leanne shook her head. "I want you to seek him out and sample his blood."

The female tilted her head to the right and asked, "To the death?"

"No," Leanne replied. "It is needed for a spell, and Guy is simply too old to render such a service to me."

Cane bared her teeth in a sneer, stating, "He should have crawled off to die long ago."

Leanne shrugged. "He serves his purpose. Perhaps when he no longer does so, you can assist him with such an endeavor."

The female let out a throaty growl that Leanne recognized as a laugh.

"I shall do as you ask, of course," Cane said after a moment.

"Excellent," Leanne said. "Now, step closer, and I shall whisper his secrets to you, and you can hunt him down at your leisure."

Cane bowed low once more, and approached Leanne, panting in her eagerness to serve.

Leanne smiled, the memories of power returning unbidden, a secret pleasure she had forgotten.

CHAPTER 10:
DECISIONS AND QUESTIONS

Ariana sat at the bar, nursing a vodka, and wondering why she was questioning her life.

Victor Daniels, she told herself, *is why I'm losing focus.*

The truth of the statement stung, and she finished her drink. From the end of the bar, the bartender glanced up, a raised eyebrow asking a silent question.

Ariana nodded, and the man walked up to her, took a bottle down from the top shelf behind the bar, and poured a double shot.

When the bartender left, Ariana glanced down into the glass at the liquor and tried to understand why she sought her answers in the bar.

Never, before her interactions with Victor Daniels, had she even needed to seek solace in alcohol. Or in anything else. She had been driven and focused, and sure of each and every action she took.

No man had ever captured her attention or even held it for more than a brief time.

Ariana was self-sufficient, as Ivan Denisovich had taught her to be.

She took a sip of her vodka and pondered the curious attraction Daniels held. Ariana didn't pity him, although she certainly felt bad about the loss of his wife and home. She had never been one for puppy dog eyes, the lost, forlorn expressions of a heartbroken man.

But then, Ariana thought, *he doesn't have those. His face is hard. There is an anger in the flesh. A hatred.*

Is that what I'm attracted to? she asked herself. *Or is it his determination?*

Ariana sighed, shook her head, and took another drink.

Her text alert sounded, and Ariana put her drink down, surprised.

She extracted the phone from an inner pocket and looked at the text.

The message was from an unknown sender.

Call her off.

There was nothing more to it.

Frowning, Ariana typed in, *Wrong number.*

Ivan Denisovich, sister. This is the right number. Tell father to call Anne off.

Surprise kept her from answering for a moment, and when she did, Ariana dimly noticed how her hands shook.

Why don't you go out and speak with her? Maybe she'll leave you alone.

Stefan Korzh's response came a moment later.

Tell him to call her off, or I'll find a way to burn the house down.

Ariana ground her teeth together and turned her phone off, jamming it back into a pocket. She picked up her vodka and drank the rest down. Her hands were steady when she placed the glass on the bar counter.

The stool next to her creaked, and she glanced over to see a young, preppie college kid leering at her. His blue polo shirt's collar was popped up, and his blonde hair was curved up in a wave away from his forehead.

"Hey there," he said, his voice low and smooth as he reached out, putting a hand on her leg. "How are you?"

Ariana's eyes flicked down to his hand, which gave her thigh a tentative squeeze, and she smiled at him.

"Thank you," she said.

"Sure," the young man grinned. "For what?"

Ariana slammed the vodka glass into his forehead, knocking the man off the stool and onto the floor, where he rolled around, moaning. Blood leaked out of small cuts, and she nodded.

"For that," she replied and turned back to the bar.

***

Stefan waited for a response to his last text. After five minutes, he decided he wasn't going to get one, so he put the phone away.

He squashed his anger, shifted his truck into drive, and pulled out of the parking lot of the grocery store. In the pickup's bed, Stefan had several boxes of non-perishable foodstuffs. Canned goods and dry goods. He also had six packages from various electronics suppliers. Supplements to the security system he had in place.

Additional ammunition had been picked up from a local sporting goods store, and he had even purchased material to make his own shotgun rounds.

Not that he had any intention of using something as bulky and as inelegant as a shotgun.

Stefan had instead decided it was time to use some heavier weaponry. The powder and steel shot he had purchased would be used for explosives. Rat poison, obtained from the hardware store, would go into them as well. A small additive that would ensure any wound created by the steel shot wouldn't be able to coagulate.

Bleeding to death will work just as well as a clean kill, he thought. His missing eye itched, and Stefan fought the urge to scratch. He had made the mistake once before, and the pain had been excruciating.

Following the ramp onto the highway, Stefan thought about the bombs he would make, the security measures that would be enhanced, and he grinned.

The plan may have hit some speed bumps, he told himself, *but I'll get it done. I always do.*

Whistling, Stefan made his way home.

CHAPTER 11

SCRATCHING THAT ITCH

Gwen's nose was sore, as was her mouth and throat. Her eyes felt puffy, her cheeks swollen. She had sobbed for hours, and she had tried to drown her fear and sorrow in wine.

Gwen lay on her bed, covers thrown off, and holding the black knife. She had the blade extended, the cool metal of the handle in her left palm. Her right index finger throbbed beneath the tight embrace of Richard's ring, the flesh around it raw from her attempts to remove the binding piece of jewelry. No matter how hard she tried, she couldn't dislodge the ring, the way it clung to her added another level of fear to her desperation.

Trying not to think about what she was planning to do, Gwen sat up, leaned forward, and placed her right hand on the floor. Clenching the knife, she took several deep breaths and brought the edge of the blade slamming down.

It stopped just a hair above the base of the finger.

Gwen pushed down on the blade, but it wouldn't budge.

"Now, now, Gwen," Richard said, his voice close to Gwen's ear. "I can't let you do that. You need to wear the ring. At all times. How else are we going to work together? That first kill was so pleasant. So *delicious,* if I'm going to be perfectly honest."

Gwen opened her mouth to answer, but nothing came out. She shuddered as a memory that was both familiar and foreign rushed to her.

The knife plunged into the young man's chest. He desperately gasped for air as his lungs were punctured repeatedly. Cutting into the young man with the care and exquisite skill of a surgeon. Removing a small section of flesh and placing it in her mouth.

She felt the texture of it, the taste, the way the fat around the meat slid down her throat.

Gwen twisted away from the memory, her attempted amputation forgotten as she dry-heaved.

"Yes," Richard murmured, "delicious, wasn't it?"

***

Ashley Hoyt finished her shift at the Moleskin Café, got herself a cup of orange flavored black tea, and waved goodbye to her regulars before she exited the building. She shivered at the chill in the night air and paused long enough to zip up her coat.

Ashley searched her pockets for her gloves and realized she had left them in the apartment. It had been warmer when she went to work, and she hadn't believed she would need them, even after her shift.

Sighing at her own foolishness, Ashley put one hand in her pocket and held her tea in the other. She had a pleasant buzz on, having enjoyed a few shots of peach schnapps right before and after the end of her shift. Her face felt warm to the touch, and she was looking forward to a bath once she got home.

Her over-sized, canvas book bag was hooked on her shoulder, and she enjoyed the sounds of the city as she turned to walk through the wide alley that would take her up to Market Street where she had parked her car.

A middle-aged, attractive woman was heading down towards the café, and she smiled at Ashley. It was a pleasant, cheerful expression, one mirrored in her eyes. She walked with a calm, self-assuredness, and there wasn't a hint of stress in the older woman.

Ashley felt herself relax. The calm that exuded from the stranger affected Ashley. She hadn't been looking forward to her shift, since she spent the better part of each day fending off the lecherous advances of middle-aged men, the clumsy come-ons from younger men, and the occasional pinch from some teen trying to show off in front of his friends.

Those men who didn't try to hit on her, get her number, or ask if she was on Tinder, were few and far between. And Ashley always appreciated them.

They passed by one another, and after a few steps the older woman said, "Excuse me."

Ashley hesitated and turned around.

The woman was holding a crumpled, twenty-dollar bill.

"I think you dropped this," she said, extending it and taking a cautious step forward.

Her eyes widened, and she shook her head, smiling. "No, thank you, though."

"Are you sure?" she asked, still holding the money out. "I mean, it looked like it fell out of your bag."

"Pretty sure," she answered.

The older woman shrugged and said, "Okay."

As she turned away, Ashley felt something warm and comforting slip over her. It was as if all of the tension eased out of her shoulders, the pain in her feet and calves were forgotten.

***

"I'm sorry," the young woman said from behind Gwen.

Gwen hesitated, the twenty-dollar bill crumpled in her hand. She could no longer sense Richard, although he had been with her only a moment before, whispering vile thoughts in her ears.

"Yes?" Gwen asked.

"I think I may have dropped it," the young woman said, taking a step closer. "It's been a long day. I work at the Moleskin Café, and some days, I'm sure you know, can be rougher than others."

Gwen nodded in agreement. "Oh, I know. Some days are just terrible."

She handed the young waitress the twenty-dollar bill and said, "Make sure you put it somewhere safe. My name's Gwen, by the way."

"Ashley," the younger woman said, putting the money away in a pocket, then shaking Gwen's hand. "Thanks again."

"You're welcome. Maybe I'll see you around sometime," Gwen said with a smile.

"You do that," Ashley said, grinning, "coffee's on me."

"Deal," Gwen said. For the first time since the morning, she felt better about life.

Sighing, Gwen started toward the mouth of the alley.

"Hey, Gwen?" Ashley called from behind her.

Gwen turned around and took a step away when a strong, firm hand closed over her mouth from behind. She tried to stamp down with her foot on where she thought the waitress' own foot would be, but the younger woman jerked Gwen's head up and down, exposing her throat. Gwen tried to twist away, but Ashley's grip tightened in her hair even as her free hand darted into her pocket.

A heartbeat later, a cold, sharp edge was pressed against her flesh.

"Such a beautiful woman, Gwen," Ashley whispered with genuine affection. "I imagine you will taste as good as you look."

The knife cut deep into her throat, and Gwen felt her own warm, precious blood spill down her neck.

CHAPTER 12:
ADVENTURE AND EXCITEMENT

Victor had managed to fall asleep in his bed rather than the chair in the study, and by doing so, he had obtained a good night's sleep. When the sun had risen, so had Victor. He had eaten breakfast alone, and he was halfway through making his travel plans when Tom walked in, yawning.

The boy rubbed his face with his hand, the left sleeve of his pajama top hanging loose. Tom only put on the prosthetic in the morning when he was going to work out first, and it still shocked Victor when he saw the empty sleeve.

"How are you doing?" he asked as Tom waved at him.

The boy shrugged and got himself a glass of water.

"Late night?" Victor asked.

"No," Tom said, putting the empty cup down on the counter. "Just tired. Bad dreams. You know?"

Victor nodded. He knew all too well about bad dreams. The nights when he managed to get through to dawn without them were few and far between, and they were to be treasured.

"Any big plans for today?" Tom asked, taking a box of Fruit Loops cereal down from a cabinet and carrying it to the table.

"I need to go up to Concord," Victor explained.

Tom's eyes widened in surprise as he sat down. Then, fumbling with the box top, he said, "Concord, Massachusetts?"

"No," Victor said, shaking his head, "Concord, New Hampshire."

"You're spending a lot of time up in the granite state," Tom said. Victor watched the boy hold the cereal box against his chest and fish a handful of the multicolored loops out. The teen ate them dry, waiting for Victor's response to his statement.

"I have to," Victor stated. "At least right now. Seems like Korzh sent another item out."

Hatred flashed through the boy's eyes, but he regained control of himself instantly. "What happened?"

Victor gave him all of the information he had been able to dig up on the internet about the ring. He watched the boy's jaw tighten, his fingers twitching.

"Do you want me to go with you?" Tom asked after a moment.

Victor shook his head. "I need you here, on the off chance that another item should show up in Fox Cat Hollow. It's unlikely, I know, but there's the possibility it could happen."

"What should I do if it does?" Tom asked. "I'm not exactly a hundred percent here, even with my prosthetic on. I'm just not that skilled with it yet."

"I need you to be my eyes and ears," Victor replied. "Read the papers. The local stuff and the ones you can find online. Make sure that you use your new name, too. If anyone asks."

Tom rolled his eyes and asked, "Why Jeremiah?"

"I don't know," Victor answered.

Tom shook his head. "I don't like it."

"You don't have to, Tom," Victor replied. "You just need to use it. Can you see if you can get Iris to call you Jeremiah in public, too? And, speaking of Iris, try to keep her out of anything that might pop up, okay?"

Tom frowned. "She won't like that. Iris does what she wants."

Victor couldn't help but smile. "I figured that. That's why I said *try*. The last I heard, Korzh is still in the area. And so is Anne Le Morte."

Tom paled slightly at the name. He had faced the doll once before at the gas station, and the boy was fully aware of how dangerous the ghost could be.

"Are you okay with that?" Victor asked.

Tom nodded, the color easing back into his cheeks.

"Good. I should be leaving in about half an hour," Victor said.

"Unless you need something from the store."

"No," Tom said. "I should be alright. Iris will come over later. If I need anything, I'll ask her to bring it. She's usually okay with that."

"I figured she would be." Victor smiled. "Okay. I'm going to finish getting my stuff together. Make sure you keep your phone on and with you, even when you're spending time with Iris."

"Yeah," Tom said, grinning. "I will."

The boy stood up, still pressing the cereal box to his chest. "Have a safe trip. You'll send me a text when you get there?"

"Of course," Victor said. "I'll talk to you soon, Tom."

The boy nodded, smiled, and left the room.

Victor sighed and tried to focus on his trip. He didn't like leaving Tom alone but bringing him to deal with another killer wasn't a priority.

The boy would be safer in Pennsylvania than New Hampshire.

***

Tom sat in his room, rubbing his left shoulder, the skin over his bicep itching at the straps of the prosthetic. It was new, a replacement for the one damaged in the fight against Molly, and the remnant of his arm was still adjusting to it. The callouses from the previous prosthetic had been in a slightly different location, and so his skin had yet to grow a new protective surface.

"Do you think it's necessary?" Tom asked, glancing over at Bontoc.

The dead man sat in the doorway to the bedroom, a gruesome specter who had taken it upon himself to help Tom.

Bontoc nodded in reply to the question, then added, "It is one thing, Tom Daniels, to allow a man or woman to remain in the afterlife. They have lived, and thus they can decide. This boy, Ezekiel, and the dog, they should go. And they should go together. He will be encouraged by you, for your kindness to him has earned his trust. The dog will comfort him, and he the dog. It is the best, though it might sting."

Tom paused, cleared his throat and asked, "How do I do it? Do I tell them to go towards the light and stuff?"

Bontoc let out a pleasant chuckle and shook his head. His face became serious as he said, "No. You will have to guide them."

"How?" Tom asked, confused.

"You must take the dog's tooth and the boy's photograph," Bontoc explained. "Hold them firmly in each hand and focus on the doorway. I have no doubt you are as strong as I believe you to be, and your strength will open a door. You may not see it, but the boy and the dog will. It will be your task to usher them through the door. Cajole them if you can, force them if you must. They have earned their peace, Tom. Let them have it."

"Will you be by the doorway?" Tom asked.

"No," Bontoc stated.

"Good," Tom said, reached over to his bedside table to retrieve the tooth and the photograph.

"Why is that good?" Bontoc inquired.

"Because I'm pretty sure you would scare the absolute hell out of them," Tom said.

Bontoc's laughter hung in the air for a moment after the dead man vanished.

Tom placed the photograph and the tooth beside him on the bed before he whispered both of their names.

Chaos arrived first, the dog trotting around the room, attempting to smell objects, although his nose could no longer perform the task. Ezekiel arrived a moment later, smiling shyly at Tom.

"Good morning, Tom," the dead boy said, crouching down to pet the dog.

"Good morning," Tom replied. He looked at them both and felt a pang of sadness. Over the short time since the ghosts had arrived in the house, Tom had come to enjoy their company. Far more than he had believed he could. Unsure as to how he should begin, he said in a hesitant voice, "I think, Ezekiel, that it's time for you and Chaos to go home."

The dead boy stood, poised to run. The hackles on the dead dog's neck rose up, and a low growl emanated from his throat.

"You don't want me here anymore?" Ezekiel's whispered question was full of pain and fear.

"That's not it at all," Tom hastened to explain. "It's just that I think it's time for you and Chaos to enjoy some peace. Rest."

The dead boy's shoulders lowered a fraction, and he asked, "I don't believe we can. We're trapped here."

Tom shook his head. "No. Not trapped. Not at all. You can go. Anytime you want. And I can help you, okay?"

Ezekiel seemed unsure of himself, chewing on his lower lip as he looked around the room.

"How do you know?" the dead boy whispered, looking up at Tom fearfully. "How can you be sure I will not go to some terrible place?"

"I don't know, not for certain," Tom confessed. "But I know that you're good, Ezekiel. And I feel that there's nothing bad waiting for you. Do you trust me?"

The dead boy's hands trembled and he nodded.

Then Ezekiel glanced at Chaos. He sank down into a squat and murmured to the dog, "Do you want to leave with me?"

The dead dog's tail wagged, and the dead boy turned his attention back to Tom. "How do we do this?"

"Hold onto my left hand," Tom said, gesturing with his prosthetic, "And I'll hold on to Chaos with my right. After that, we'll all focus on the doorway, okay?"

Ezekiel looked doubtful, but still, he nodded. As the dead boy stood up and grasped Tom's false hand, Tom put his living hand into the cold, insubstantial aura that was Chaos.

"Ready?" Tom whispered.

Ezekiel nodded, and the dog let out a whimper as if he could understand and answer the question as well.

"Okay," Tom said, looking at the door, "let's do this."

He kept his attention firmly on the doorway and he was surprised to see a curious gray light spill into the bedroom.

Warmth replaced the cold both the dead boy and dead dog had exuded, and Tom felt Chaos slip out of his grasp as Ezekiel stepped away.

Fearful of shattering whatever was happening, Tom remained silent, even after the boy and dog passed through the doorway, and the world shifted back to reality.

The light in the room was dull, a pale imitation of what had been on the other side of the veils.

Exhaustion swept over him and a moment later, Bontoc appeared in the room.

"Did I do that?" Tom asked in hoarse whisper.

"A little, though not much, my friend," Bontoc replied. "What you did was convince Ezekiel that he could leave, and that was far more important than the seed of ability that lies within you. As you grow, you will achieve more, and learn more, as do we all. Rest now, Tom Daniels, and be well."

Bontoc offered his grim smile and vanished from the room.

Tom felt an overwhelming sense of sadness, and he realized, dully, that he was crying. Wiping the tears away with the back of his hand, he stretched out on his bed, closed his eyes, and wept for his parents.

CHAPTER 13:
POWER CORRUPTS

===

She heard the blow before she saw it.

Leanne twisted on the seat, her head moving a fraction of an inch as a heavy blade slammed into the ornate back of the seat. Her hand lashed out, and dark, crackling energy surged from her fingertips.

A voice rose up in a scream, and a tall, thin human male stumbled away from the dais. The energy wrapped around him, the stench of seared flesh stinging her nose as the power from her fingers burrowed into his eyes and open mouth.

His skin erupted in tiny geysers of energy, dark spouts leaping forward to fall back and dance on his ravaged face.

When he collapsed, Leanne stood and let her hand fall to her side.

In silence, she strode down the dais to stand beside the dead human. His features were unrecognizable, looking more like a pot of gumbo than a face. The curious, bitter stench of burnt hair hung in the air, and she glanced around her.

No one else could be seen.

She was alone.

Leanne bent down, pried open the dead man's mouth and tore out his tongue with a swift jerk. She bit off a small section of the limp flesh, swallowed it and whispered, "Speak answers to my questions."

The body on the ground before her shuddered.

"Who are you?" she asked.

"Daniel Gibson," the dead man answered.

"Whose servant were you?" Leanne asked.

"Hers," he answered.

"Her name?" Leanne demanded.

"Leanne Le Monde," the dead man replied.

She straightened up, surprised.

The dead couldn't lie. Not to her. And not when she had partaken of the tongue. It was old magic, the best kind. Bloody and raw. An easy spell to cast, but one that required power to see it through.

Someone had given the servant to her, but without her knowledge.

"And to whom did you belong before?" Leanne asked.

Before he could answer, the dead man shuddered, and his body collapsed in upon itself. His flesh turned to dust, as did the tongue in her hand.

Anger spiked within her as she brushed the remnants of flesh from her hands. She straightened up and looked around her, eyes searching the shadows for some sign.

There was nothing to see.

Glowering, Leanne stalked back to the seat and sat down angrily upon it. She waited for several minutes until her temper had settled, and then called out to the guard.

A young lycanthrope sprinted into the room. He bowed low and asked, "Elder, your command?"

"Bring him and his family to me," Leanne said in a low voice.

"Yes," the guard said, bowing again. The lycanthrope knew of whom she spoke.

"And send me the cook as well," Leanne added.

The guard nodded and hastened out of the room.

Less than a minute later a portly goblin hurried into the room, panting and out of breath.

"Elder?" the goblin said, his voice thick with the accent of his kind.

"Do you prepare fish here, Cook?" she asked.

He nodded. "Would you like some, Elder?"

"No," Leanne said. "She would not. What she would like is your filleting knife."

"I have two," the cook replied, "which would you prefer?"

"Bring them both," she answered as the first of the man's family arrived. "I have a suspicion I will dull the blades before the night is through."

CHAPTER 14

ON THE TABLE

Detective Sara Milton stood in the medical examiner's autopsy room and ignored the stench of chemical cleaners as best she could. The two recent murder victims were stretched out on a pair of tables beside one another. Large, brutal 'Y's defiled each individual's chest and thick stitches kept the dead flesh together. The knife wounds, the bite marks, and the slashed throats were all bound in the same manner.

Sara couldn't help but notice that each victim's injuries were disturbingly similar.

Gil Hurston came into the room, put his coffee mug down on a counter, and nodded good morning to her. The mug, Sara saw, stated Gil was the 'World's Best Dad'. She wondered if his kids knew he used the mug when he was cutting into murder victims.

"How are you this morning, Detective?" Gil asked.

"Tired," Sara answered. "And hungry."

"You should have eaten," Gil chided her.

"If I had, one of your staff would be cleaning my vomit up right now," she stated.

"No," Gil replied. "That's what the hoses and drain are for."

It was an old bit they did. Gil knew she wouldn't eat, and she knew he'd mention the drainage system. The repetition of the old tit for tat had a calming effect on her stomach, which always found the sight of a body on the table to be decidedly unpleasant.

Sara could deal with them in the street, in a car, a bed, somewhere in the wild. Anywhere but the cold sterility of the medical examiner's autopsy room.

It felt like a desecration to her. A final act of humiliation against the victim, and she despised it.

"I take it this is the work of one person?" Sara asked, forcing herself to concentrate on the two victims.

"Yes," Gil replied. "Same wound depth. Same removal pattern for a part of the breast meat. Even the same manner in which the throat was cut. It seems like their heads were jerked back, exposing the throat to the blade. I dusted the faces for fingerprints. I sent the results off to the lab and forwarded the prints to the FBI's database as well. Just in case our killer isn't a local."

"Do you know if the killer's male or female?" she asked. Sarah agreed with the assumption, but she wanted to know why Gil thought so.

"Could be either. There were a few strands of hair left on each victim of each gender," he answered. "Once we test it a little more, we'll be able to build a pair of complete profiles."

Sara turned away from the bodies. She was used to corpses. They didn't bother her too much in general, but the savage way the victims had been butchered made her skin crawl.

Gil picked up his mug and together they left the room, retreating to his small office. His desk was cluttered with papers, knickknacks, and three or four Dunkin Donuts cups. Books were crammed into shelves around him, and white and black binders were stacked on top of one another. The man was short and stocky, and as unkempt as his office. Despite his appearance, Sara knew Gil's mind was exceptionally sharp. And his eyes, though bespectacled, didn't miss anything.

She sank into the battered chair across from his desk as he eased down into his own, the frayed and pale green vinyl held together with silver duct tape.

"Don't you get a line in your budget for office supplies?" she asked.

"Sure," Gil replied. "Spend it on binders. And ink for the copier. Doesn't matter how many emails I send you guys the lawyers always want something printed out. Drives me nuts. I mean, I'm not a tree-hugging hippy, but come on, Sara, I'm pretty sure I've deforested entire sections of Maine just to keep the Attorney General happy."

"Damn," she said, leaning back. "Maybe they should get a bust of you and put it somewhere. You'd probably employ a whole town."

"Ha ha," he said, smirking, "you've got some jokes, Detective."

"I have to," she said, her humor fading. "I'm not having any luck with the case."

She jerked her thumb behind her towards the autopsy room.

Gil nodded. "I wish I had more for you."

"I know, and I appreciate it," Sara said. "Anyway, we're going through all of the closed-circuit tape we can get our hands on. That's about the only good thing that's come out of all the opioid-related crime lately. Lots of shops putting in cameras. Some of it's only triggered by motion sensors, but hey, something's better than nothing."

"I'm a little nervous," Gil said after a moment.

Sara frowned and asked, "Why?"

He gestured toward a framed photograph on his desk.

Sara leaned forward and held back a groan. In the picture, Gil was flanked by two daughters on his right, and a third daughter and his wife on the left.

"Oh Gil," Sara said softly, "I'm sorry."

He nodded. When he spoke, it was with some difficulty, his voice breaking.

"I keep telling them not to go out alone, and I really, really hope they listen to me," he said. "They're a little headstrong. Think they can take on the world. Love that about my girls. I do, but hell, Sara, whoever did this, they're not worried about anyone. Not a soul. They did these in alleys. And not in the dead of night. The killers don't care."

The last words were spoken with a father's concern, and Sara had a hard time looking at him.

She shook her head and stood up. "You keep telling your girls not to go out alone, Gil. I'm going to go and hunt the bastard who did this."

Sara closed the door as she left, and she forced herself to look at the bodies again.

No more bodies, she thought, leaving the room. *None.*

CHAPTER 15

BACK IN NEW HAMPSHIRE

Victor checked into his hotel room, left his bags unpacked, and went out to the hardware store. Once there, he wandered around until he found the plumbing section, and picked out a foot-long length of cast iron pipe. From the safety aisle, he selected a pair of mechanic's gloves, the palms, and fingers coated with rubber to give him a surer grip on the pipe. Holding his items, he walked to the roofing department and found a scrap of lead flashing for the roof. He grunted at the weight of the item, but he carried everything to the self-checkout and purchased his supplies with cash.

Soon enough he was back in his hotel room with a meal from KFC and his items. With the television on in the background for noise, Victor ate, then twisted and shaped the lead into a rough envelope. Large enough, he hoped, to hold the possessed ring if he happened to be fortunate enough to acquire it.

Finished, Victor sat back and looked out the window at the city skyline.

The hotel room's phone rang, the sharp jangle jerking him upright.

Surprised, Victor turned off the television and answered the phone.

"Hello?" he asked hesitantly.

"Victor," Ariana said, "what brings you back to the Granite State? Seriously, you spend an awful lot of time here."

Victor carried the phone to the window and searched the parking lot.

"Are you here?" he asked.

"In your room?" Her tone was teasing and cheerful. "I think you may need glasses, Victor. And no, I'm not. Close enough to be, but not quite. You know the deal."

"Yes," Victor replied, closing the shades and walking back to the bed. "I believe I'm well aware of the deal at this point. Why are you calling, Ariana?"

She hesitated a moment before she coughed and answered.

"Same old, same old," she said, the jovialness in her voice sounding slightly forced. "Wondering why you aren't in Pennsylvania. Why aren't you hunting my darling brother?"

Victor sat down, the mattress sinking slightly beneath his weight, and swung his legs up onto the bedspread.

"I'll get to him in my own time," Victor answered. "This is a little more important."

She laughed, and he could hear her open a bottle. The sound of liquid pouring into a glass was clear and distinct over the line. "You found out there's another one of my family's items here."

"I did," Victor said. He picked up the television remote, thumbed the power button on, and muted the volume. Victor scrolled through the channels until he found the weather station and left it there, watching the following day's forecast absently.

"Is it really so important?" Ariana asked.

"Of course," Victor replied. "The ring needs to be contained. There are two dead people. I wouldn't be able to look at myself in the mirror if I allowed it to continue."

"There's an easier solution," Ariana said, a note of bitterness in her voice.

"What's that?" Victor asked.

"Don't look in any mirrors," she said, the words cold and harsh. "Don't forget, Victor Daniels, all of my father's special conquests were horrific. This one is no less. We know what he did in the United States, but no one is quite sure how many he killed and mutilated in Vietnam. I admire your courage and your convictions. I would honestly hate to see you slain because of them. Be careful, Victor. And, as they say, don't trust anyone."

Before Victor could offer a reply, she hung up. He held the receiver a moment longer, then placed it in the cradle. Pressing the mute button, the volume sprang into existence, and Victor settled in to see what sort of weather he would be hunting in.

CHAPTER 16

ABUSED AND MISUSED

Oliver finished the angry retort he had written to eBay customer service, reread it, and then sent it along with a furious click of his mouse.

Neither the seller nor eBay was offering him any sort of recompense for his financial loss.

Ridiculous! he fumed, pushing himself away from the desk and getting to his feet. Oliver stomped into the kitchen and only lightened his tread when Mrs. Purvis from the floor below, struck the ceiling with her broom handle.

Not only is the ring gone, but the money, too! He opened the refrigerator, took out a bottle of rose wine, and poured himself a large glass. With the cool drink in his hand, Oliver returned to his computer, sitting down again. In silence, he drank the wine, and when he made it half-way through the glass, he leaned forward and created a fresh document. His fingers flew across the keyboard, and a smile spread across his face.

Dear Haunted49Alpha,

I am certain you have been informed by eBay that they believe I have no substantive claim against you. My attorney, however, disagrees with eBay's legal team and has advised me to file suit. Soon I shall have your real name, address, and phone number. When this is done, I will be able to bring you to a small claims court here in New Hampshire, and we will resolve this issue in the court system.

I could not help but notice that the shipping originated in Pennsylvania when I was tracking the package online. You need to ask yourself if a forced trip from Pennsylvania is worth refunding me my money. I am quite certain you will spend a far more significant amount of funds merely getting to New Hampshire and defending yourself than the price I paid for the stolen item.

Against my lawyer's wishes, I am advising you to remain in Pennsylvania and to merely refund me.

Chortling with pleasure, Oliver read the letter over several times, made a few slight adjustments, then sent it racing along the mysterious highways and byways of the internet.

That, Oliver thought, finishing his drink and feeling tipsy as he stood, *should solve that problem.*

Humming to himself, Oliver returned to the kitchen, refilled his glass, and again wandered back to his computer. He felt so certain that he had won his point against the nameless seller, that he logged onto eBay, and began a search for Norwich University items.

***

Stefan Korzh reassembled his pistol, checked the action on the weapon, and placed it down on the table in front of him. The soothing, familiar act was a balm for his troubled mind.

Beyond the fence of his compound, Anne Le Morte and her companion roamed the woods. He had seen tracks earlier in the morning during a quick reconnaissance of the perimeter. And there was an itch at the base of his skull as if someone watched him.

The sensation irritated him and reminded him of how he had kept a wary eye out for both his parents when he was a child. His father's lessons, more often than not, were punctuated with a slap. At least from the age of ten to thirteen, when Stefan was supposed to be learning how to seek out the dead, and not turn them loose onto the world or each other.

Stefan smirked at the memory of the first gladiatorial combat he had arranged between a pair of the dead.

But the smirk vanished when the notification for his email chimed.

He put the pistol on the table and clicked on the mail icon.

It was another email from the buyer in New Hampshire.

Stefan opened the mail, read it once, then twice, and then a third time.

When he turned the computer off a moment later, he felt anger twist in his stomach. He didn't know if the man was telling the truth, or if he was speaking falsely.

The point, Stefan realized, was that the man was threatening him.

And Stefan didn't like to be threatened.

The idea that the buyer's lawyer could find a way to compel him to travel to New Hampshire made him understand that he would have little in the way of satisfaction, even if he won.

No, Stefan thought, tapping his fingers on the desk. *If I get summoned to New Hampshire, there won't be any way I can punish him.*

Sighing, Stefan stood up. *I'll need to take care of it soon. Before it gets out of hand.*

But not before this place is as secure as possible, Stefan thought. *Not until I know Anne Le Morte can't get in.*

CHAPTER 17:
AN UNPLEASANT AND UNSETTLING SENSATION

It seemed almost a cliché to Tom as he stood in the living room and looked out onto the street. He had developed the bad habit of cracking the knuckles on his remaining hand, bending each finger down with his thumb until the corresponding joint popped. There was no real sense of relief, and Iris hated it.

Tom found himself cracking them as he eyed the dog across the street.

The animal was huge. Larger than any he had seen in person before. It seemed to be a cross breed between an Irish Wolfhound and a British Mastiff.

The dog's fur was long and coarse, its eyes a curious green, and Tom could see the nostrils flaring in the streetlight's glow. It sat upright and watched him through the window. He knew he wasn't imagining it. If he stepped to the left, the dog's head moved with him. The same if he stepped to the right.

Tom had even left the room and gone out to look at the sidelight on the front door, only to find the dog's attention focused firmly upon it.

The cellphone pinged, and he dug it out of his back pocket. He read the text, a quick update from his mobile carrier, and then looked back at the dog and let out a surprised yell.

The dog had crossed the street.

It sat in the front yard, mouth open a fraction of an inch, the tongue protruding from it. There was a sense of raw power and violence to the animal. As if it were waiting for the right moment to spring through the air and shatter the window.

Tom knew it could. He knew it wanted to.

Something held the dog back. And the idea that it could actively consider the act was frightening. A deep intelligence lurked behind the green eyes, and Tom wondered if the dog was there for him, or for Victor.

The thought that it might be for Victor Daniels chased any sense of fear out of Tom.

Anger replaced the void, and he heard his blood pound in his ears. He stomped back to the front door, twisted the knob and jerked it open. A spike of pleasure arose within him as he saw the dog take a quick, unexpected step back.

But that joy was short lived as the animal quickly recovered.

A mixture of anger and fear swirled within Tom as the dog's hackles rose and it stared at him. It bared its teeth, the lips curling back and a low, guttural growl emanated from its throat.

"Get off the property." Tom's tone was flat and even. None of the fear he felt tainted it, nor did any of his anger. He was in control, and his spirit soared with that knowledge.

The dog's growl shifted into an abrupt bark that sounded almost like a laugh, and when the sound had died, a soft, pleasant voice said, "I'll go. Tell the one I want I'll be back for him."

Tom watched as the dog turned its back to him and trotted away, tail wagging back and forth lazily.

It took him almost a full minute to understand that the voice had, undeniably, come from the dog.

CHAPTER 18:
ON THE PROWL

Rules and regulations.

They served to protect not only the people of Concord but the officers who enforced them.

Rules were important. They raised humanity above the level of animals.

Detective Sara Milton chewed on a piece of gum meditatively, her hands in her pockets as she wandered along Main Street. The sun had set, and the decorative streetlamps cast their pleasant light upon the sidewalks and pavement. Traffic flowed along, people on their way to various points in their lives. Sara found an empty bench and sat down on it, crossing her legs and admiring the city.

Her thoughts cleared, her rhythmic chewing slowed, and she felt herself slip away. It was a comforting sensation, drifting into the contemplative state that allowed her to focus on her problems.

And the two murders qualified as problems.

The similarities in the crimes were glaring, and the fact that the killings happened so close to one another was unnerving.

Sara felt an edge of worry creep back into her thoughts, so she let it enter, and then pass through. She knew that worrying didn't help solve any problems. It only increased them.

The murders had been kept out of the Concord Monitor, and off WMUR News out of Manchester. But that would only last so long. The media made their money by telling the news, and editors and writers alike were eager to get their hands on the story.

Sara knew that someone would eventually bring up the term 'serial killer', and that would make life unbearable. Panic would rise up in the community, and the killer could go into hiding.

Or at least stop killing for a while, Sara thought. But that wasn't a good option, and she knew it. The killer would go right back to it as soon as they could, or if they had the financial capability, they might pack up and move. And while that would remove the people of Concord from the killer's direct influence, it would only be shunting the problem off to another community.

The killer has to be caught, Sara thought, *and it has to be here.*

She sat for a few more minutes, then sighed and got to her feet. Both of the victims had lived nearby, and Sara felt it was time to visit some of the different restaurants and shops. Just to mingle and see if anyone she knew had been hanging around and causing trouble.

Or even if they just had a bad feeling about one of them, Sara thought. *It doesn't take much more than that sometimes.*

Stuffing her hands back into her pockets, Sara made her way to where the victim had been found.

***

Richard admired the woman as she walked away. Her face was attractive, with a high forehead and fierce cheekbones above a thin-lipped mouth. She walked with a purpose, and Richard appreciated that. He too moved with a purpose, although he doubted his and the woman's goals were the same.

Richard watched her for a moment longer, then turned around and made for a nearby alley. He followed her to the next street, whistling to himself. Several restaurants had kitchen doors that opened onto the alley, and Richard waved to those cooks and busboys he saw. A few waved back, but others were far more intent upon preparing some meal.

He appreciated their dedication.

Like them, he was intent on preparing a meal as well.

Earlier in the day, he had discovered a fine shop named Kaffee mit Schlag, and as he purchased a cup of coffee, he had seen an attractive blonde waitress.

Richard turned right out of the alley, and a few steps more carried him to the front of the shop. He entered and was greeted by the same waitress he had seen earlier. His heart gave a rapid flutter as he returned the greeting.

Richard sat down at a table and waited for the waitress to come back for his order. She did so a minute later, smiling at him with perfect, white teeth.

"Guten Tag," she said, giving him a playful wink, "My name's Heather, and I'll be your waitress. What can I get for you today?"

"I'm Ashley," he said, remembering his current victim's name and returning the waitress' smile, "I'd like a tall coffee, light on the cream, heavy on the sugar. And, if you have it, I would love a piece of coffee cake."

"I can do that," she said, jotting his order down on a small notepad. "I'll have them back to you in a jiffy, Ashley."

"Thank you," he replied and watched her walk away. His fingers twitched, and the knife clipped to the inside of his pocket grew heavy with his anticipation.

***

Sara had turned left onto Franklin Street off North Main and walked into the German coffee shop. Walking up to the counter, she waited a moment until Phil, the barista, glanced up at her.

"Hey," he said, grinning, the silver gauges in his earlobes flashing in the shop's subdued lighting. "How are you?"

"Good," Sara said. "Is the German in today?"

Phil shook his head. "No. Yeltsin's on vacation this week."

Sara looked at him in surprise. "He left someone else in charge of the shop?"

"Yeah, I know," Phil said, brushing a stray lock of his bright blue hair out of his face. "I think he had a stroke, but he won't admit it."

Heather, one of Yeltsin's tried and true employees, came out of the kitchen area with a tall cup of coffee and a piece of coffee cake thick enough to sink a battleship.

"Hey Sara," Heather said, "how are you?"

"Good," Sara answered. "Got a minute?"

"Sure," Heather said. "I just need to bring these out, and I'll be right back."

"Coffee?" Phil asked.

Sara shook her head. "Hot chocolate, please. Can't have any caffeine after midday. Doctor's orders."

"Cool," Phil said. "Take a seat, and I'll bring it over when it's ready."

"Thanks," Sara said. She strolled away from the counter, took an empty table in the far corner of the room so she could watch the entrance and the windows that looked out onto Franklin Street.

Heather joined her a moment later.

"So," Heather said, concern flashing across her face, "what's going on?"

"I wanted to ask you if there's been anyone in lately who's given you a bad feeling," Sara asked, her voice low.

"Nothing too creepy," Heather said, matching Sara's volume. "Why?"

Sara hesitated a moment, then decided to be truthful with the young woman. "We've had a little bit of violence against some wait staff. Locals who you might have known."

Heather's face paled, and her brown eyes widened. "Oh my God. Who?"

"I can't tell you that right now," Sara said, trying to say it gently. "But I want you to be careful and keep your eyes open. Don't leave work alone, and if you get a bad feeling, about anyone, man or woman, I want you to call for a cop."

"Oh, come on," Heather whispered, and Sara could see panic building in the young woman's face.

"Hey," Sara said, hardening her voice, "Look at me."

When the waitress did so, Sara said, "Pay attention. *Don't* leave work alone. That's all you have to do. Understand?"

Heather nodded. She swallowed, cleared her throat, and asked, "Are you telling everyone?"

"Yes," Sara said. "As many as I can. The more of you guys out there, watching and listening, the better chance we'll have of grabbing the individual before anything else happens."

Phil brought the hot chocolate over, and he glanced worriedly at Heather.

"Thanks," Sara said, accepting the drink. "Take Heather out back for a moment. Let her catch her breath."

Phil didn't ask. Instead, he whispered something to Heather and helped the young woman to her feet.

Sara wrapped her hands around the hot porcelain of the mug and let it warm her. She glanced around the coffee shop and saw a pair of young men, their heads bent close as they discussed some secret fervently. A young woman sat beside the door, the monstrously large piece of coffee cake Heather had been carrying in front of her.

As Sara drank her hot chocolate, her attention kept drifting back to the young woman. Her clothes were nondescript, as was her face, and she ate and drank with precision as if she had spent years in the military, or in the violent confines of a prison.

But she looked too young for either.

Movement to her right brought Sara's attention back to the two young men, both of whom had separated. Their attention was now focused on their individual cell phones. A glance at Phil showed he had his out as well, and Sara imagined Heather was occupied with the same in back.

It reminded her to check her own phone. She had turned the volume down before she had entered the shop. With her hand on the phone, Sara froze.

***

Richard felt the woman's eyes upon him and knew she suspected him. It was a gut instinct, and he listened to it. Standing up, he took the money roll out of Ashley's front pocket. He peeled a twenty off the top, placed it beneath the heavy porcelain of his coffee mug. Returning the roll to the safety of his pants, Richard exited the shop without a backward glance, the sound of a chair's legs scraping across the floor following him out.

He turned to the left, then left again into an alley, and broke into a run. A recessed doorway appeared on the left after a dumpster which he threw himself into, pressing himself back.

***

Sara stood on Franklin Street, her phone to her ear.

"Navi," she said when Navi Shaara answered his phone.

"Sara," he started, but she cut him off.

"Send a couple of cruisers down to Kaffee mit Schlag," she said hastily. "I think I spotted our killer."

Sara gave a brief description of the woman from the shop and then ended the call. She wandered up to the left and saw several alleys that branched off. Her shoulders sank.

She's gone, she thought bitterly. *I'll have to send the cars up to State Street and hope she hasn't gotten too far.*

Angry, Sara called Navi back and had him correct the course of the dispatched vehicles.

***

Richard remained in his hiding place, the acoustics of the alley allowing him to clearly hear the woman's side of the conversation each time she used her phone. Eventually, a car pulled up, and she got into it, leaving him undisturbed.

Richard was disappointed that she had figured him out, but

disappointment was a significant part of both life and death.

Smiling, Richard removed a pint of whiskey from his inner pocket and took a long swallow. He had plenty of time to sit and wait.

Heather's shift would end sooner or later, and he desperately wanted to speak with her.

Although he thought, grinning, *the conversation will be a trifle one-sided.*

CHAPTER 19:
BALANCING FAMILY AND WORK

She stood before the house, unsure as to whether or not she should enter. In the sagging structure in front of her, Ariana understood that her father had raised a son and remained married to his wife. An old pain rose up within her heart, the sadness of not fully understanding why her father chose to stay with a wife he disliked, and a son who disappointed him.

Her own mother had worshipped the ground Ivan Denisovich had walked upon, and that devotion had transferred itself to Ariana. Yet while she had tolerated the situation, Ariana had never truly embraced it.

Enough reminiscing, she scolded herself. Ariana climbed the weathered and worn stairs to the porch, the boards of which creaked and groaned beneath even her slight weight. When she reached the door, it swung open of its own accord, the house silent as she stepped in.

"Greetings, Ariana, daughter of Ivan Denisovich," a man's voice said. "We welcome you to his home."

The air had the bitter chill she had expected, but the speaker had caught her off guard. Ariana had not believed any of the dead would have welcomed her.

"Hello," Ariana said, keeping her attention on the hall in front of her as the door clicked shut. "Did my father tell you to expect me?"

"Of course," the stranger said, chuckling. A shadow separated from the far wall, yet it did not form into a definitive shape. Instead, it remained a mere hint of a body, and she wasn't sure if it were by choice, or a lack of strength. Knowing the type of ghosts her father and his wife had collected, Ariana suspected it was a matter of choice.

"Would you care to explore the house for a bit?" the dead man asked, a curious, anticipatory note in his voice.

The question made her skin crawl, and Ariana stated, "No."

"Ah," the man said, sounding genuinely disappointed. "A pity, that. There are so many dark places to share with you here."

"Would my father appreciate these places?" Ariana asked in a flat voice.

The dead man let out a nervous chuckle. "Ah, no. No, he would not. In fact, Ivan Denisovich Korzh would be exceptionally displeased with me."

"Then why risk it?" Her curiosity was piqued.

"It has been a long time, young lady," the dead man said in a hoarse whisper, "since I've wrapped my fingers around a woman's throat. You cannot blame a man for trying."

"I believe my father could," she replied.

"And he does." Ivan Denisovich's voice rolled down the stairs at the end of the hallway, and the shadow she had spoken with vanished.

"Come to the second floor, daughter of mine," her father called, joy thick in his voice. "Pay no heed to the dead loitering my halls. I am pleased you have come, although I do not know why you have made the trip."

"I have a question for you, father," she replied, making her way to the stairs and climbing them quickly.

"One you could not ask from the comfort of your own home?" he inquired. "This sounds ominous, my dear daughter."

When she reached the landing, Ariana hesitated and asked, "Where are you?"

"Look at the doors." His chuckle filled the air as he added, "And tell me which room you think I might be in."

A door off to the right was locked and bound with iron, and Ariana walked to it.

From the other side came the sounds of voices, many speaking in tongues she had never heard before.

Her father's own, deep voice came from beyond, the words rich with pleasure.

"Now, tell me, my dear child," he said, "What brings you here, to me?"

"It is Victor Daniels," she replied, keeping her tone light and hiding the tremor that had begun to appear whenever she thought of the man.

"Ah, the widower of one of your brother's first victims," Ivan Denisovich said.

"Yes," Ariana answered. "I know that you've sworn him off from helping us, but I'd like to bring him in. See if he'll agree to help us find Stefan."

"And why is that?"

"I'm not fully recovered yet," she admitted. "Attempting to challenge Stefan by myself would be foolish."

"But you are not alone, dear child," Ivan Denisovich said, chuckling. "You have more than capable assistance in the form of Anne Le Morte."

"I would have to disagree with you there, father," Ariana stated. "I think the only living person Anne was willing to assist was Bontoc, and he's dead. If I go and seek her help, I'm almost positive she'll kill me out of hand."

Ivan Denisovich was silent for several minutes, and Ariana waited as patiently as she could.

"She is a rebellious sort. So be it. Get his agreement," her father said, his voice losing some of its jovialness. "Stefan is a problem that needs to be solved, and quickly. Speak with Victor Daniels and tell him I shall not kill him for assisting to apprehend my wayward son."

"Thank you, father," Ariana said.

Her father said, "I know where your thoughts are headed. Despite the setback concerning Bontoc, I do not wish for Victor Daniels to kill my son, even if the opportunity arises. Nor should you wish for him to murder your brother, regardless of the injury he caused you. This vengeance is ours. Not others."

Ivan Denisovich paused and then added, "Is that understood?"

"Yes," Ariana said.

"Excellent, now, you shall go to Victor Daniels and gain his agreement?" her father asked.

"Yes. I'll speak with him," Ariana said.

"Excellent. Now, sit, my dear, and speak with me," her father said.

She sat down on the floor outside of his room, ignoring the dust and dirt of time scattered around the floor. "What do you want to talk about?"

"I am dead," Ivan Denisovich replied, "but that does not preclude me from being concerned with my progeny. Or his future."

Ariana frowned. "What do you mean?"

"Grandchildren, Ariana," Ivan Denisovich said, laughing. "When will you bless your father with grandchildren?"

Ariana felt her face go red, and she found herself at a loss for words.

CHAPTER 20:

QUESTIONS WITHOUT ANSWERS

"What the hell was it?" Tom asked, sliding Bontoc's ring off his finger and placing it on his dresser.

Bontoc sat on the floor in the bedroom, his grisly appearance relegated to the realm of mild distraction.

"Describe it again, Tom Daniels," the dead man said.

Tom did so, quoting what the dog had said.

"It sounds to me," Bontoc said, after a few minutes of silence, "that it is a creature not of this world."

"What do you mean?" Tom asked, confused. "Another ghost, like you?"

The dead man shook his head. "By no means. I am of this world. Or rather, I was. It is not unusual for the dead to come back in some way. But this, this is unusual. This sounds almost otherworldly. More like, what is it? Ah, yes, a fairy tale. Some creature of legend, yes?"

"A fairy tale animal?" Tom asked.

"No?" Bontoc asked. "I admit, I was a bit taken aback myself, but I have, as is said, put my ear to the ground. I have seen a world beyond our own. Even beyond the one I am in now. I have caught glimpses of Western fairies and Eastern dragons. I have seen the Kapre and the Tiyanak of my own people. These creatures of myth, of legend, Tom, they are everywhere."

"That's a little hard for me," Tom said, shaking his head.

Bontoc laughed, and Tom looked at him in surprise.

"Really, Tom Daniels?" Bontoc asked, still chuckling. "And yet here you are, on your bed with an arm missing, destroyed by the cold touch of a possessed doll. Here I am, on the floor in front of you. I am dead.

Murdered by Stefan Korzh, who in turn caused the death of your parents before me. And look upon me, Tom Daniels. Look at the form in which I return. Bloody and torn, a misshapen ghost, albeit with my head still attached. Now, think of these things, and tell me, is it truly so hard to accept the fact that creatures from fairy tales might walk with us?"

"No," Tom whispered. "Jean Luc."

Bontoc tilted his head and looked at him, asking, "Who is this Jean Luc?"

Tom quickly told him the story of Jean Luc and the death of the goblin.

When he finished, Bontoc's face was fixed with a serious, dangerous expression.

"This creature is here about Jean Luc." The dead man's statement was spoken in a hard and firm voice.

"How do you know?" Tom asked.

"I do not know," Bontoc said, "But I suspect. It is the only rational explanation. I believe it would be best for you to go into the basement, where you buried Nicholas' mug in the salt. He is the one who slew this goblin. Perhaps he will be able to tell you more about this creature you saw. But you must take care. Remember, this man has no true affection for you. You were merely a means to an end."

"I will be," Tom said, getting to his feet. He snatched his iron ring off the dresser and slipped it onto his finger as he hurried out of the room, Bontoc keeping pace easily beside him. Tom flicked on the lights, raced down the basement stairs and went to the far, dark corner where he and Iris had hidden Nicholas' mug.

The entire bucket was missing.

"Oh no," Tom said, twisting around and looking desperately in the other corners.

"He's gone?" Bontoc asked.

"Gone," Tom said, fighting the fear rising in him. The doorbell rang and Tom nearly jumped.

Faintly, he heard someone call his name.

"I'll be back," he said hastily to the dead man.

"I have all of the time in the world, my friend," Bontoc called after him.

Tom hurried up the stairs, and by the time he reached the first floor, the person at the front door was pounding on it.

"Tom!" Iris yelled.

Fear spurred him into a run, and Tom twisted the doorknob and jerked the door open.

Iris stumbled in, her face a shade paler than normal, her eyes wide with fear. She tore the door out of his hand and slammed it shut, her fingers fumbling at the lock.

"What is it?" he asked. "What's wrong?"

"There's a dog or something out there." Her voice shook as she spoke. "It was the biggest animal I've ever seen. I thought it was a bear at first. But then, when I got a good look at its face, I realized it wasn't. You need to call someone!"

"He already has," Bontoc said from behind them, and when Iris looked up, she screamed and pushed herself closer to Tom.

"Ah," Bontoc said, grinning, "I am quite the mess, am I not, fair Iris?"

But before anyone could respond to his question, something scratched at the door.

***

A fine mixture of exhaustion, rage, and desperation had settled over Stefan, and it had begun to cloud his thoughts. Carrying his rifle loosely, he picked his way through the razed landscape around his fencing. The day before he had hired a company to come in and remove every bit of growth that had crept up to the fence. Stefan had spent the morning installing the new cameras and sensors, and then he had gone out on foot to see what tracks could be found.

There had been precious little.

Whoever was assisting Anne Le Morte was either more skilled at woodcraft than the previous caretaker, or far luckier.

Either way, Stefan thought, nearing the entrance to his compound, *I'm out of luck. At least for today.*

When he reached the gate, he paused, checked that the area was clear, and hastily entered the code. Soon he was on the other side of the fence, feet firmly planted on the cracked asphalt of the parking lot.

His heart rate, which had been far too high for the better part of the day, slowed down enough to let him feel comfortable, and he felt a small grin appear on his face as the gate slid closed.

The small hairs on the back of his neck stood up, and the grin vanished.

Stefan could feel eyes upon him.

He tightened his grip on the rifle but kept it where it was. His lone eye scanned the woods and found the watcher.

From where he stood, the individual looked to be more shadow than flesh, but Stefan knew it was nothing more than a trick of the light. He didn't stare at the person, not wanting to give away the information that he was aware of the stranger's presence.

Once he had the stranger's position fixed, he turned his back to the individual and took several steps towards the structure before he spun on one heel and dropped to a knee. He fired off three quick shots before he saw that the stranger was no longer there.

For a full minute, he remained in that position, ready to fire again.

But the stranger didn't reappear.

Finally, disgusted, Stefan stood, left the brass casings on the asphalt, and returned to his makeshift home.

***

"Will you open the door, Tom?" Bontoc asked.

"No," Tom answered, his voice firm. "I am not going to open the door."

"We cannot deal with this stranger if you do not," the dead man stated.

"Why not?" Iris demanded.

"Because," Bontoc replied, "we should get what answers we can, and it would be rude to try and get them with a door separating us."

Tom considered the statement, and then he thought about cowering in the house. He looked at Iris and asked in a soft voice, "Do you want to leave?"

The line of her jaw tightened, but she shook her head.

"Okay," Tom whispered. He let go of Iris and opened the door.

He stepped back, a deep, primal fear swelling within him at the sight of the giant beast on the doorstep.

It looked from Tom to Iris, and then its eyes came to rest upon Bontoc.

And as they watched, the creature shifted its form in front of them.

A tall, vaguely humanoid body took shape. Coarse, dark hair covering a female figure. The face continued to bear a dog-like semblance, with an elongated snout and wide-set eyes. When the lips curled back, in either a grin or a sneer, the teeth revealed were definitely canine. Yellowed and brutal in appearance.

Her voice, when she spoke, was regal and undeniably proud.

"My name is Cane," she stated, "and I bring greetings from the Elder. I am here to escort Victor Daniels to stand before her."

"I thought I had told you to leave," Tom said, his voice shaking slightly.

"And so you did," Cane replied. "And my liege bade me to return, and to bring a hostage to her."

Before Tom could ask her what she meant, Cane lashed out, and his world went dark.

CHAPTER 21

A LITTLE EXTRA BUSINESS

Heather wasn't headstrong, or foolish.

But she did tend to be forgetful.

It wasn't until she had finished her shift and was halfway to the parking garage that she remembered the detective's admonition that she not go out alone.

A tendril of fear found its way into her heart, but Heather had taken a few hits off Phil's bong before she had left, and all felt right with the world.

She tried to focus on what exactly she was supposed to keep an eye out for, yet every time she thought she had it, the information slipped away, leaving her with a flurry of giggles.

Maybe I had a little too much, she thought, bursting into laughter.

"Hello," a voice said, and Heather looked up.

***

Dazed and disorientated, Ashley stumbled, tripped over her own feet and almost fell.

A gentle, but firm hand caught her by the bicep and held her upright.

Confused, she looked at her Good Samaritan and found a face vaguely familiar. She squinted, smiled, and asked, "Do I know you from somewhere?"

"I work at a German coffee shop," the young woman replied, guiding her up the street. "I waited on you earlier."

"You did?" Ashley asked, walking tiredly. "I'm sorry. I'm not feeling well, and I don't remember much of today."

"That's alright," the stranger said. "What's your name?"

"Ashley," she answered. "Are you a waitress?"

"Yes," the young woman replied. "And my name's Heather."

"Nice to meet you, Heather," Ashley said. "I'm a waitress, too. God, some days I think I wait on a hundred people."

"Feels like more than some days," Heather confided, turning and helping Ashley walk up a slim alley.

"You know, I never believed my mom," Ashley said. "She was a waitress for years. I can remember her coming home in tears some days, her feet swollen in the cheap tennis shoes she wore."

"Oh my God," Heather said, "I have gel inserts in my sneakers, and they're worth their weight in gold. I can't imagine being in a pair of flats for a whole shift."

"Well, as you know," Ashley said, "Being on your feet all day is difficult. And when she could find a babysitter, she would pull a double."

"Wow," Heather said in an impressed tone.

"Yeah," Ashley agreed. "You know, I've only worked a double once, and it just about killed me."

"The doubles won't kill you," Heather said, patting Ashley's hand gently.

"No?" Ashley enjoyed the curious scent of marijuana and sweat that formed an aura around the other young woman. Feeling playful, she asked, "What will?"

"I will," Heather said with a wink, and something cold, hard, and sharp slipped between Ashley's ribs.

***

The sounds of sirens jarred Victor out of a light sleep and forced him from the comfort of his bed. He staggered to the window of his hotel room, pulled the curtains back and tried to pinpoint where the noise came from.

The room's phone rang, and he groaned as he went and answered it.

"Ariana," he said, yawning.

"Did I wake you?" she asked.

"What time is it?" Victor asked in return.

"Two in the morning," she answered.

"No," he said, sitting on the bed and rubbing his eyes with his free hand.

She laughed and asked, "Then why did you want to know the time?"

"Because I didn't know." He yawned again. "Two calls in two days. What's the occasion?"

"Have you found the ring?" she asked.

"No," he replied, "I have not."

"I'd like to offer my assistance then."

The statement surprised him into silence.

"I know you're there," she said a moment later. "I can hear you breathing. And usually, it's supposed to be the person who calls that doesn't talk and just sort of breathes all creepily into the phone."

"Yes, well," Victor said, trying to gather his thoughts, "the offer is a little surprising."

"You know that I don't want to kill you," Ariana said.

"No," Victor conceded, "but your brother doesn't seem to have an issue with it. And last time I saw your father, he said he'd kill me if I interfered."

"Well, even dear old Dad's had a change of heart," she said. "In fact, we were hoping you'd be willing to help us apprehend Stefan, and sooner rather than later. And for that to happen, I need to help you wrap up the mess that Stefan's seemed to have made here. So, the offer is here, would you like my help?"

He thought about it for a moment, and then the sirens grew louder.

"I hear them, too," Ariana said, "And I can tell you, it's nothing good. Chatter on the scanner is that another body has been found.

Female. Mid-twenties. And in an alley. Sound familiar?"

"Yes," Victor whispered.

"Why don't you sleep on it?" Ariana asked. "I'll call your room at nine. If you answer, then we can get together and hash out the details. If not, we can figure it out from there."

"Sure," Victor said. "Goodnight."

"Goodnight," she replied.

After he had hung up the phone, Victor sat in silence on the bed. Beyond the walls of the hotel, the wail of emergency vehicles continued.

What choice do I have? he asked himself. There was no answer, and in silence, he lay back down and hoped sleep would return.

***

Sara put a piece of gum in her mouth and walked up the short alley to where the crime scene unit had cordoned off a large segment. She stopped short of the cordon and blinked in the glare of the powerful lights that stood on yellow tripods and illuminated the murdered girl.

The body belonged to a young woman named Ashley from one of the coffee shops, and she had been butchered in the same fashion as the others. And it was the same woman she had tried to stop from the coffee shop.

From what Sara could see, there was less blood.

Frowning, she called one of the forensic techs over and asked her, "Less blood than the first two?"

The tech, whose name Sara couldn't recall, gave a nod. "He killed her quick. Looks like a single puncture into the ribs from the left. Don't quote me on it, but that's the consensus here. He took his time with her body, though. There's a lot more, um, desecration, I guess you could call it."

"That bad?" Sara asked.

"Yeah," the tech said, "That bad. You know, oh damn, detective, it's like he was cutting the choicest pieces out."

The tech shook her head, grimacing. Without another word, the woman went back to her job, leaving Sara alone and looking at the handiwork of the killer.

That's three now, Sara thought. *Three. And he's got his routine down.*

He's done this before.

Chewing her gum furiously, Sara walked back the way she had come. It was time to get back to the station and see what she could dig up online about the serial killer operating in Concord.

CHAPTER 22:
TRAVELING

Stefan Korzh's fury caused his teeth to ache and his head to pound.

He had received another email from the purchaser of the class ring. The one who wanted his money back.

And shipping too, Stefan snarled, *let's not forget that little tidbit.*

He slammed his overnight bag down onto the table and began to stuff it with clothes. A few toiletries followed, and then he zipped the bag closed with a jerk. Shouldering it, he snatched his car keys off the rack and stormed out of his quarters. The door clicked and locked behind him, and a moment later, he was in the plain, brown Ford Taurus that served as one of his cars. The engine turned over easily, and Stefan left the warehouse as quickly as all of his security precautions would allow.

Soon he was on the road, the sun cresting the horizon. He stopped a few minutes out of town and got himself a coffee at a gas station that looked as if it hadn't been remodeled since the early 1980s.

Stefan settled himself in, buckled his seatbelt and turned on the radio. It took him a short time to find a station that wasn't broadcasting news or sports and headed toward the interstate.

He needed to get to New York, where he would switch cars. Then he would repeat the process in Massachusetts before he drove up to Concord, New Hampshire.

He needed to find Oliver, the man who had decided to threaten him with legal action and kill him.

The idea of murdering the man helped Stefan to calm down, and it put a smile on his face. He imagined how pleasant it would be to watch the man die.

Maybe I'll hurt him a bit first, Stefan thought. Then he shrugged. *I guess that depends on traffic. If it's bad, well, then I'll take out my frustrations.*

And traffic was terrible before he even left Pennsylvania.

***

Tom was decidedly uncomfortable when he woke up. His left arm throbbed where the prosthetic was attached, a painful reminder as to why it was best to take it off before he laid down to rest.

His mouth was dry as he sat up, yawned, and tried to remember how he had gotten home.

As he looked around, he had the terrifying realization that he wasn't home.

And that he hadn't taken a nap.

He was in a small courtyard, and he looked out upon it through the bars of a cage. A glance up showed he could stand upright, and he did so.

In the darkened courtyard, he saw figures move, flitting from one deep shadow to another. A short distance away he saw a dais, and on it was a single, large and ornately carved chair.

From where he stood, Tom saw a slight figure seated there, a woman who watched him intently.

He beat back a rising sense of panic and forced himself to concentrate and to ignore the fact that he was imprisoned.

Slowly, Tom counted to one hundred. When the woman still hadn't spoken to him, he turned around and sat down, his back to her.

The stranger's laughter filled the air, and she stated, "Well done, young man. You neither railed nor raged against your new situation. Nor did you demand an explanation."

The woman's voice was familiar.

Tom twisted around in time to see her stand and step down from the dais. Her steps were smooth, each movement fluid and with an economy of motion that was exceptional for its grace and elegance.

"Tell me, Tom Daniels," she said, coming to a stop a few feet away from him, "how do you think your new father will react to your absence?"

"Not well," Tom answered. "Is Iris here?"

"The girl who was with you?" the stranger asked.

Tom nodded, not trusting himself to answer.

"No," the woman said in a gentle tone. "Holding her would have no effect upon Victor. She was, from what Cane told me, rather put out by your capture and removal, and had the dead man not calmed her down, my hunter might have been forced to kill her."

Tom repressed a shudder of rage and remained silent, focusing on the fact that Iris was alive and with Bontoc. He could only hope it was a better situation than the one he currently found himself in.

"You're a quiet young man," the woman said, stepping closer. Details emerged, and he was surprised at how beautiful she was, and at the way her ears had a curious point to them. And he was struck by the familiarity of it. "There's something about you. A special quality. Did you know that, Tom Daniels?"

"Do I know you?" he asked after a moment.

She smiled. "No. Not truly. We met once before, and that was more in passing than anything else. I do know Victor Daniels, and it seems that the only way I might have the discussion I want with him is to have you as my hostage."

"Who are you?" Tom asked.

"I am Leanne Le Monde," the woman replied, her voice gentle.

"What?" Confusion swept through him. "Victor said you were old. Jeremy said you were like two hundred."

"Far, far older than that," Leanne said, lowering her voice to a whisper. "I was old when I found my way here with the first Irish who fled the famine. And I will be old when the last of your kind withers and dies. More importantly, I will discuss with Victor Daniels, the death of a loyal friend. And that discussion will take place here, at my own seat of power. Do you understand, Tom Daniels?"

Tom thought about the question for a moment, nodded and replied, "Yes. Good luck with that."

She raised an eyebrow and asked, "And what do you mean by that?"

"He's a little rougher now," Tom answered as he stretched out on the rough floor of his cage. "And a whole lot angrier. I don't know if you'll want to talk to him. Even here."

Her appreciative chuckle filled his ears as Tom closed his eyes.

"We will see, young man," she said, and Tom listened to the soft tread of her feet as she walked away from the cage.

CHAPTER 23

HEATHER CAN'T CATCH A BREAK

When Heather woke up, she wasn't home.

She didn't know where she was.

Groaning, she crawled out of the corner she found herself in and moved into the center of the room. There was an old carpet beneath her, a faded, putrid green that stank worse than it looked. She could smell urine and vomit, and something small and foul had died in it recently. Out of the corner of her eye, she saw a brown mass that may have been a rat or a mouse at one point, but now it served only as a breeding ground for the maggots that writhed in its rancid flesh.

"Oh God," Heather whispered and vomited a steaming pool of half-digested meat and alcohol onto the carpet.

With a whimper, she retreated back to the corner and pressed her forehead against the cool wall.

"I take it you're not feeling well this afternoon?" someone asked from across the room.

It took her a moment to remember the night before, the bizarre fever dream in which she had spoken with a dead man. A killer named Richard who had used her to murder a woman, and to dine upon her corpse.

"No," Heather moaned. "Please, leave me alone."

Richard chuckled and said, "No. That's not in the cards. We're bound together now, Heather. I have no intention of letting go of you. I am having entirely too much fun."

"How can this be fun?" Heather asked. "You tortured me last night!"

"You?!" Richard asked, his voice filled with incredulity. His laughter roared in Heather's ears. "You have no idea as to what torture is, Heather. None. Can you fathom the amount of blood on that knife now tucked in your pocket? No, you cannot. They aren't quite dead, you know, when I cut into their chests. The last one, a delightful young woman named Ashley, she was quite aware of what I was doing when I popped a piece of her into my mouth and chewed it. Perhaps, next time, I'll take a larger piece. We'll bring it back to this hovel and cook it up on that excuse of a stove. Do you have any idea as to how delectable a piece of flesh is when fried in butter?"

"Please," Heather begged. "Stop."

"No," Richard said, a gleeful note in his voice. The dead man manifested a few feet from her. "I won't. And neither will you. As I said, there's no way to separate us now. We may as well be conjoined twins since you're wearing my ring."

Confused, Heather looked down at her hands and saw a large, dull silver ring on her right index finger.

"I'll cut my finger off!" Heather exclaimed. She fumbled at the knife in her pocket, expecting the ghost to try and stop her at any moment. Yet Richard didn't move. Instead, the dead man watched her with what seemed like bored detachment.

Heather managed to get the blade open, holding it above the knuckle of her index finger.

"I'll cut it off," she whispered.

Richard grinned at her.

"No one, dear Heather," the dead man said, "is trying to stop you. So please, continue. Cut off the offending finger."

She bit her lip, and her hand shook as she lowered the blade until it was a hair's breadth above her own flesh. Her eyes flickered towards Richard, whose grin remained in place.

Heather tried to push down, tried to force the steel into her own flesh.

But she couldn't.

Richard wasn't stopping her.

Sobbing, Heather threw the knife down and collapsed to the floor, curling into a fetal position and closing her eyes so that she wouldn't see the mocking sympathy on the dead man's face.

"Now, now, Heather," Richard said in a soothing tone, the chill from the ghost wrapping around her. "You needn't weep so. You're a coward, and there's little you can do about that. Who knows if it is a fault of breeding or education, but it is undeniable nonetheless. Accept it. No, embrace it. Allow yourself to sink into that true freedom, the freedom of being able to blame your actions upon that of another. In this case, I am your scapegoat. It is a role I take on willingly, if not humbly. Do you understand?"

Heather whimpered and gave a nod.

"Excellent," Richard cooed. "Now, you'll find a bottle of rotgut whiskey by the door. Take it, drink it, and let us be about my business."

With a shudder, Heather forced herself out of her fetal position, and like a worm, she crawled toward the door.

***

A knock on the door woke Sara up. She lay on her back on an old army cot, staring up at the drop ceiling in the supply closet and trying not to wince at the crack of light that came in through the slightly open door.

"You alright, Sara?" Meg Loveless asked.

"Hell no," Sara said with a grunt, sitting up. "What's going on?"

"I have coffee for you. You've been in there for about six hours," Meg replied.

"Okay, come in," Sara said, rubbing her face.

The other detective stepped in quickly, closing the door over to keep as much of the light out as possible. She held out a paper cup of coffee, and Sara accepted it gratefully. The coffee was strong and bitter, and hot. Exactly what she needed.

"You awake?" Meg asked.

"No," Sara grumbled, "but I'm close enough."

"Good," Meg said, "these came in for you a little while ago."

Sara accepted a sheaf of fax paper and glanced at the top page.

All vestiges of sleep fell away as she saw the modus operandi of Concord's serial killer described on the page. Her eyes scanned all of the information and then came to a sudden stop.

The killer, one Richard H. Bronte, Norwich University, Class of 1967, was dead. Lynched by a group of Arapaho Indians in 1976 after he had attempted to cut up a young woman on their reservation.

"This has to be a copycat," Sara said after a short silence.

"Yeah," Meg agreed. "But how in the hell would they pick out this one? And why?"

Sara shook her head. "Who knows why the crazy ones do anything? Anyway, thanks for bringing this in."

Meg nodded. "We were able to gather up some video feeds from the local businesses."

"Anything?" Sara asked, trying not to allow her hopes to rise.

They did anyway, and they were dashed all the same when Meg replied, "Nothing definitive. The killer can be seen. We can even watch when she picks her off the street."

"She?" Sara asked, surprised. She knew female serial killers existed, but she felt genuine shock at Meg's statement.

Meg nodded. "She. The victim."

"The victim," Sara repeated, confused. "You're telling me Heather killed this woman?"

"Yeah," Meg said with a sigh.

"Did she fight or scream or anything?" Sara asked, already knowing the answer.

"No," Meg said. "She went willingly into the alley with her. Hell, Sara, she was even leaning on her."

Sara took a sip of the coffee, put the sheaf of papers on the cot beside her. "She knew Heather?"

"Maybe," Meg said.

Frustrated, Sara drank the rest of her coffee, ignoring the liquid's painful heat, and stood up.

"Alright," she said as Meg opened the door, "let's go see if we can find where Heather is."

The two women left the supply closet, their anger filling the air around them.

CHAPTER 24:
GETTING HIS MONEY'S WORTH

Saturday found Oliver irritated and ready for the day to be over, even though the sun had only been up for a few hours.

He had received an email from another seller on eBay that his package had been delayed due to a family emergency. There was still no information from the seller of the Norwich ring, and when he had reached his car to go to the gym, Oliver had discovered a large leak beneath it. An hour later he had watched his new Audi A4 be driven out of the parking garage on the back of a flatbed tow-truck.

The radiator, according to the grease-covered tow-truck operator, had sprung a leak.

Oliver had called the dealership, but he had learned, much to his chagrin, that no one was going to be in the service center until after nine.

A miserable, nasty day, Oliver thought, slumped on the couch and furious.

He glanced at the clock above the television and saw he had twenty-seven minutes before he could call.

A secretary had taken his message, and she had assured him that someone would call him promptly at nine, but Oliver didn't believe her.

No one, as far as he was concerned, ever did anything promptly.

It was a sad, simple fact of life.

And then his phone rang.

Surprised, Oliver picked up his telephone and looked at the caller ID; he saw the Audi Dealership's general number.

"Hello?" he asked, unable to keep the pleased shock out of his voice.

"Mr. Prescott?" a man asked in a cheerful voice. "I hear you called earlier? Your Audi is here with a radiator issue."

"Yes, that's right," Oliver said, standing up and bracing himself for the argument.

"I'm terribly sorry that you've had to endure such a difficult start to your morning," the man continued. "I can tell you that we are working on your radiator right now, and, from what my technician tells me, we'll have your car ready for you in about three hours. Now, if you need to go anywhere, I can send someone over with a courtesy vehicle, and we can get you in one of the dealership's newest vehicles."

Oliver let out a laugh and said, "Ah, no. No, I don't need to go anywhere."

"Well, if you change your mind, you can certainly call us here. Otherwise, I'd like to have someone pick you up at around ten if that works for you," the gentleman said.

"That would be fine," Oliver replied. "I'm not going anywhere. Just have your driver ring the bell in my building. Either I'll open the door or the super will."

"Excellent, thank you very much for your patronage, Mr. Prescott," the man said cheerfully, "and we'll see you soon."

Still shocked and pleased, Oliver ended the call and set the phone down on the dining table. As he did so, there was a gentle, timid knock on the door.

Smiling, Oliver had a spring in his step as he walked over, undid the deadbolt, and opened the door as much as the security chain would allow.

A man dressed in a green utility uniform, with a baseball cap that read, *Willette's Pest Services*, stood on the welcome mat.

As Oliver opened his mouth to ask what the workman wanted, the stranger lifted a gloved hand and sprayed Oliver in the face. A brutal, horrific burning sensation filled his mouth, eyes, and nose. Stumbling backward, he struck the dining table, fell to his hands and knees and began to vomit.

There was the sound of a soft clink, then the clatter of the security chain dropping. Through a film of tears, Oliver saw the door open, and then close with a click. The deadbolt was thrown, and when Oliver tried to speak, he threw up instead.

Long streams of mucus mingled with bile and the strawberry protein shake he had had for breakfast dripped from his mouth.

A heartbeat later, the stranger grabbed Oliver by the hair and dragged him along the floor. Gasping and sobbing, Oliver tried to keep pace, crawling along the floor.

Soon, the carpet beneath his hands was replaced by the tile of the bathroom floor.

"In," the stranger said, jerking Oliver up.

"What?" Oliver asked, the word painful to speak.

"The tub. Get in."

As Oliver scrambled over the dimly seen side of the tub, panic filled him.

He recognized the voice.

It was the man from the Audi dealership.

"Hands," the man said.

"What?" Oliver asked again.

Instead of repeating the question, the stranger sprayed Oliver in the face again.

Gagging and coughing, he couldn't resist as cold metal snapped around first one wrist, then the other, and his hands were pulled above his head. A pair of loud, cold clicks filled the close confines of the bathroom, and Oliver understood he had been handcuffed to the shower's handles.

Fear overtook him, and he struggled against the metal, trying to grab hold of the side of the tub.

But it was no use and the brief surge of energy that the adrenaline had given him vanished, leaving him exhausted and wheezing.

"Keep your mouth shut," the stranger said, "or I'll be back to cut your tongue out and feed it to you."

The calm, dispassionate tone convinced Oliver of the man's sincerity.

Cowering in the bathtub, he waited while the stranger left the room and came back in less than a minute.

Oliver's vision slowly returned, and he watched as a large, black duffel bag was opened. Various cleaning chemicals were removed and set on the floor, and as the stranger emptied the bag, Oliver stole looks at the man, trying to remember his features for when he could report the assault to the police.

The stranger's face was expressionless, but he wore a black patch over his left eye. His features were plain, and his head was shaved from what Oliver could see. The man's hands were hidden by thick, dark blue latex gloves, and the hat and uniform, while neat and clean, were well-worn. Even the man's work-boots, which were a scuffed and faded black, were unremarkable.

No one, Oliver realized, would look twice at the man on the street.

Or if he were to walk out of Oliver's apartment on a Saturday morning.

The man's eye-patch might be noticed, but most would forget it, not wanting to appear to be staring at someone's injury.

"What do you want from me?" Oliver whispered.

The man didn't answer him.

Instead, the stranger took a pair of medical scissors out of the bag and turned to the tub. He held the scissors in his right hand, and what looked to be a container of pepper-spray in the other.

Oliver repeated his question as the stranger brought the scissors closer.

Panicking, he opened his mouth to scream, and the man sprayed Oliver again.

Gagging and shuddering, Oliver couldn't resist as the stranger methodically cut all Oliver's clothes off.

Naked in the tub, Oliver began to sob.

The stranger put the scissors and the pepper-spray down on the floor. From the bag, he took a roll of duct tape and quickly used it and a scrap of Oliver's t-shirt to make a gag.

"Now, Oliver Prescott the fourth," the stranger said, retrieving a small, propane torch from the bag, "you and I are going to discuss the Norwich class ring you ordered from me."

Oliver let out a moan and tried again to twist free, tearing the flesh on his wrists until blood came streaming down his upraised forearms.

The stranger lit the torch, adjusted the flame, so it was a bright, unhealthy blue, and smiled at Oliver.

"This is going to be a long, in-depth talk," the man confided, "because you have made me exceptionally angry, and I have had to come a long, long way to do this. So, I want you to know, I'm going to make it worth my while."

Oliver fainted as the torch neared him.

But he came howling back to consciousness as the flame bit deeply into the soft flesh of his underarm.

CHAPTER 25

TIRED AND FULFILLED

Stefan Korzh sat on the toilet seat and stared at the burned and bloody mess that served as the earthly remains of one Oliver Prescott IV.

The man had died quickly, and not from Stefan's work with the propane torch.

Oliver had been a coward, and he had willed himself to die.

That had been at shortly past eleven in the morning.

Stefan had worked on the man for another five hours, and he had enjoyed every minute of the work.

He had packed up his tools, and the used propane bottles. The handcuffs had been soaked in bleach and ammonia, and they would be thrown out somewhere along a back road far from the city of Concord, New Hampshire.

Stefan looked at the bottles of chemicals on the floor, all of them caustic. They would not react with one another when combined, but they would render the meat and bone and sinew of Oliver Prescott IV to nothing more than a murky stew in the bathtub.

Stefan had purchased them one at a time at different stores on his trip up from Pennsylvania. The bottles would be left for the police, but only after he had scrubbed them.

An earlier reconnaissance of the apartment had yielded the dead man's vacuum cleaner, which Stefan would use on his way out of the apartment. It would go with him, like the handcuffs, and eventually end up on some back road, or in a pond. Not as a single unit, however.

Stefan would disassemble it as he went, tossing a piece out here, and a piece out there.

"You cost me a lot of time and effort," Stefan said casually to the corpse.

The man did not answer him, and Stefan was pleased about that. There was always a chance, albeit a slim one, that he might kill someone and the individual's ghost would remain behind. And while he had dealt with a great many ghosts over the decades, Stefan had never been confronted by one he had personally crafted.

He shook his head and got to his feet. He still had a good deal of cleaning left to do, and it wouldn't get done with him sitting in the bathroom admiring his own handiwork.

Stefan scratched at the edge of his eye-patch, careful not to get the gore-splattered latex glove near the still healing injury. He paused in front of the bathroom mirror, observed that he appeared as though he had stepped out of a charnel house, and made a mental note to clean up before he left the apartment.

Whistling, Stefan squatted down, opened up the duffel bag, and took out a pair of plastic booties to put over his own footwear.

It was time to erase every trace of himself from the apartment.

The cleaning, he knew, would be restful. A calming, peaceful act to help him prepare for the long trip home.

***

Ariana had eaten a light dinner and left her car parked at the hotel Victor was staying at. She had attempted to see him, but when she had knocked on his door, the man hadn't answered.

Just as well, she thought, strolling along the sidewalk. *I have more time to think now.*

She still felt as though she was going at the entire business with Victor the wrong way. There was the uncomfortable flutter in her stomach when she thought of him, a feeling that only increased when she spoke with him on the phone. The memory of it caused her to frown, and to chastise herself for such a juvenile reaction to the man.

Chemicals, she scolded herself. *Only chemicals. There's something about him that's triggering your pheromones. Stop it.*

Telling herself the reason why her body was reacting in such a way didn't stop it from continuing.

She turned onto Franklin Street, vaguely aware that she was retracing the steps of the latest victim. Pausing at the intersection, Ariana waited for the light to change, her eyes following traffic as it rolled by.

Her eyes fixed on a large, flat white Econo-line van labeled *Willette's Pest Services*. She looked at the driver hunched over the wheel, a baseball hat pulled low and a ridiculous eye-patch over his left eye.

But as the vehicle turned away, she saw the rest of the man's face reflected in the side mirror.

It was her brother.

She felt a chill sweep through her, and she stared at the vehicle.

Ariana didn't bother to try and get the license plate number. It, or the vehicle, or both, would have been stolen.

And while she was certain he had committed a crime in the city of Concord, she had no idea as to what it might be, or why it had been done. Two essential ingredients for the police to sit up and take any sort of notice.

She did take out her phone, and she dialed a number she was surprised she knew by heart.

"Hello," Victor Daniels said.

"Stefan's here," she said.

The inhalation of Victor's breath was sharp and crisp over the phone. "In Concord?"

"That's where we are," she snapped and then got herself under control. "I'm sorry. Yes. He's driving in a large white van. I don't know if he's coming or going, although I suspect the van is going."

"Why?" Victor asked.

"Just a feeling," Ariana replied, watching the van take a left and vanish from sight. "Listen, I don't think he's here for you. And I know he's not here for me. But just to be on the safe side, don't go out for a bit. Stay wherever you are."

"I just got back to my room," he said. "So, I'll order some room service and sit tight."

"Alright," Ariana said. "I'll be there in a few minutes."

She hung up the phone and put it away, and only when she was in the act of crossing the street did she realize she had invited herself to the man's room.

It sure isn't a date, she told herself.

But a small part of her wished it was.

***

Before he could ask why, Victor found himself holding his phone and listening to a dial tone.

He felt uncomfortable with the idea of Ariana coming to his room. It was a mixture, he knew, of her being the daughter of Ivan Denisovich and the fact that she wasn't Erin.

But Stefan Korzh was no one to be trifled with, and Ariana would be more than helpful should her brother appear suddenly at the door.

Resigning himself to the visit, Victor picked up the room service menu and ordered a simple steak and eggs dinner. In a short amount of time, the meal arrived, and he had just begun to cut into the steak when his phone rang again.

When he answered it, Ariana stated, "I'm outside your door."

Victor put the cell phone down, stood up and went to let her in.

She sat down at the table across from his seat, reached out and picked a home-fry off his plate and popped it into her mouth.

Victor sat down and took a sip of water before he asked, "Did you see him again?"

Ariana shook her head. "No. Do you have a scanner?"

"A scanner?" Victor asked, confused. "What do you mean?"

"For the police band," Ariana replied, taking her cell phone out and setting it on the table.

"No," Victor said with a surprised chuckle. He took a bite of egg and said, "You can't get a scanner. It's illegal."

"Lots of things are illegal," Ariana said with a shrug. She pressed an app on her phone, keyed in a code, and then adjusted the volume. A male voice came across, speaking a numerical code and a street address.

"Scanners are illegal," she continued, "but that doesn't stop people from making apps that can access the digital broadcasts. I'm pretty sure if we listen in long enough, we'll hear why Stefan was in Concord. It's a little too suspicious, considering you're here too."

"And what about you?" Victor asked. "Isn't it a little odd that you're in the state as well?"

"I'm just plain odd," she said with a wink, "and if that doesn't answer your question, then nothing will."

Victor went to speak again, but the scanner interrupted him. He caught the name of an address, and Ariana let out a snort of laughter.

"What?" Victor asked, trying to eat his dinner.

"Someone's about to get arrested for drunk and disorderly conduct," she explained. "That's what a 10-59 is. Well, the drunk part is. I can only assume disorderly is going to be tacked on once they arrive on the scene. It usually is."

"Do you listen to scanners a lot?" Victor asked.

"Whenever I can," Ariana answered.

Victor realized she was serious, and he asked, "Why would you?"

"I do a lot of work that requires me to know what the codes are," she said shortly, giving him a shy smile. "And knowing what the codes are, and who is responding to them and where they're responding to makes my job easier."

"Can you share what your job is?" Victor felt as though he didn't want the answer, but at the same time, he was compelled to ask.

"Before Stefan hurt me," she said slowly, "I used to hurt people. A lot of people. For a lot of money. My father taught me some excellent skills, Victor. Unfortunately, most of them can't be used in a polite setting."

Victor wanted to tell her that what she had done was wrong. That what she would probably continue to do was wrong.

And then he thought about his own actions since Erin's death, and he found he couldn't pass judgment on the woman.

The chatter of the scanner filled the silence that rose up between them.

CHAPTER 26:

IN DARKNESS DEEP

Tom had no sense of time, and he discovered he was bothered by that.

He lay on his side, staring out at the dais and the creature that was Leanne Le Monde. Earlier he had been awakened by her voice raised in anger, but the words were unintelligible and had stopped almost as soon as he had heard them.

Whatever she had said sent those around her scurrying for safety.

A short time later, a snuffling sound came from behind him, and Tom jerked around to see the luminescent eyes of Cane staring at him. The female beast squatted and watched him, her nostrils flaring.

Tom felt his anger rise at having been taken prisoner by her, but he stifled it and asked, "Is there something you want?"

She bared her teeth in what he hoped was a grin, and asked, "How did you lose your arm?"

He considered, for a moment, telling her the same joke he had used about the cat scratching him, but then he thought it might be in poor taste. And poor taste might result in some sort of physical repercussion he wouldn't be able to avoid or respond to. Tom thought about a well-crafted lie, and then decided that it would be easier to tell the beast the truth. And so he did.

He told her everything about the gas station, Iris, Bontoc, and Anne Le Morte.

When he finished, Tom was sitting up, his back against the bars of the cage and to the dais.

Cane was no longer squatting but sitting cross-legged. She tilted her head to one side and said, "Well done."

Tom found himself grinning, and he asked, "What do you mean?"

"I can smell courage on you as easily as I can smell a lie, Tom Daniels," Cane replied. "I know that you speak the truth. In fact, from your scent, I know you do not add all that there is, and that is in an effort to not appear boastful. It is a pity that you and I have had to meet like this."

Tom shrugged, and he tried to hold back the sense of pride that swelled within him.

"Thanks," he managed to finally say, keeping his voice even.

The female chuckled.

"Were you older," she said, getting to her feet and stretching languidly, "I would challenge your female for you. But you are a pup still, and there is time to wait."

By the time her words registered, Cane had gone back into the darkness, leaving him with red cheeks in the cage.

Before he could think much more about her comments, Tom was distracted by a commotion from the dais.

He got to his feet and turned around in time to see a pair of human slaves carrying a large box between them. They set it down in front of the dais, then hurried away as Leanne stood and stepped down to the box. She opened the lid with a flick of her wrist, and a scream exploded from the contents.

Stars popped along the edges of Tom's vision, and he staggered back as far as his confinement would allow him.

Over the scream, he heard Leanne's voice as she spoke a single word.

"Silence."

And the scream was cut off.

"Get out before I drag you out," she added and returned to her seat.

A dark shape climbed out of the box, took a step forward becoming defined in the emerging light.

Tom shuddered with rage and fear as he recognized Nicholas, the ghost he had sought to destroy.

The one who had vanished from the basement.

Nicholas seemed to sense Tom, and he turned around, taking one long step towards the cage.

Leanne closed her right hand into a fist, and Nicholas shrieked, collapsing to his knees.

Tom hadn't believed that a ghost as vicious and deadly as Victor's grandfather could look frightened and beaten. Seeing the dead man's behavior made Tom a believer.

Nicholas remained on his knees, head bowed, and when Leanne spoke, she did so in a voice that carried across the small, open area.

"Do you know where you are?" she asked.

Nicholas shook his head.

"Speak!" a goblin shouted and reached forward and slammed an unknown object into the ghost.

It didn't pass through the dead man but struck him instead. A burst of light ripped through the court and Nicholas screamed. The smell of burnt fabric filled the air and Tom repressed a shudder of fear.

"No," Nicholas hissed, "I do not know why I am here."

"Liar." Leanne chuckled and shook her head. "You know why you're here. You murdered my friend. An old and trusted comrade who I had the good fortune to rescue. I kept him close and then lent him to assist in the hunt for Korzh. And you murdered him."

Nicholas didn't respond to the accusation.

"At first," Leanne continued, "I believed that Victor Daniels was the one to blame and that Jeremy Rhinehart had been but a pawn in the event. How surprised I was to learn that both Jeremy and Victor had been mere pieces in your game."

Nicholas' chin lifted up slightly, and a defiant note entered his voice as he declared, "I need a body, and both my grandson and Jeremy blocked that."

Leanne made a small gesture, and the goblin that had struck Nicholas before, did so again.

Another ear-piercing scream was wrenched from Nicholas' dead throat as he collapsed to the ground. The goblin kicked him repeatedly until the ghost got back to his knees.

Tom shook his head, unable to understand how Nicholas could be so beaten.

"The rules are different here," a voice whispered behind him, just a few inches from his ear.

Tom jerked around and saw Cane standing behind him.

She flashed her feral grin and added, "The rules of your world are not entirely the rules of our own. Time is different, flesh is different, the spirit is different. When they are above, and in their proper forms, most of our kin are unable to confront the dead physically. They are weaker, in that regard. Jean Luc was such a one. Had he not been, well, we wouldn't be discussing this in the first place. Now, while we cannot all strike the dead, there are certain members who can. Montcalm is the goblin's name, and he possesses that unique ability. He enjoys it."

Tom glanced at the goblin and saw Cane had stated the truth. There was a malicious smile on the creature's face, and he seemed to long for the chance to strike Nicholas again.

"Do you want to know peace?" Leanne asked.

"No!" Nicholas spat.

"Good," she said, reclining in her chair. "Then we are in agreement. I don't want you to know it either. You believe you have suffered all you can at my hands, and in the world above, that is a fine and definitive truth. Here, that is not the case."

Leanne leaned forward and smiled at him. "Here, Nicholas, there is so much more I can do to you. And I will."

She gestured once more, and Montcalm advanced on the dead man.

Within moments, Nicholas' agonized shrieks filled the heavy air.

CHAPTER 27:
FEAR AND SELF-LOATHING

Heather sat in the darkness of the bathroom, head bent over the toilet and a bottle of mouthwash in her hands.

With mechanical motions, she removed the cap, brought the mouth of the bottle up to her lips, and took a small sip. She rinsed with it, then spit into the toilet.

Richard's ring was an oppressive weight on her hand, and Heather wished she had the ability to remove it.

You know how you can take it off, she reprimanded herself.

But she couldn't do it. Not sober. And if she was drunk, she knew she would weep over the whole situation. The idea of cutting her finger off to remove the ring caused her stomach to tremble, and Heather whimpered, afraid she might throw up again.

I just want to die, she thought, tears streaming from the corners of her eyes. *That's all. That's it. Nothing else matters.*

Flashes of memories had been rising up within her. Horrific scenes of mutilation and death. And she had done them. Or at least her body had, and her eyes had acted as recorders.

From beyond the closed bathroom door came the sound of humming.

Richard was moving around the apartment, happy and pleased with the torture he had visited not only upon the girl he had killed but on Heather as well.

Please, Heather prayed, *please let me die.*

"Heather," Richard said from the other side of the door, "I think it's time you come out of there. There's work to be done."

"No," she whispered.

"Oh, Heather," Richard said, suddenly in the room. "That wasn't a request. It was a command."

Heather howled as she tried to get away from the dead man, but Richard's cold, pain-inflicting hands wrapped around her wrists and began to squeeze.

"Now," Richard said in a conversational tone, "get out there and drink."

Weeping, Heather did so.

***

Sara held a poor photograph of Heather in her hand.

The image wasn't as defined as she would have liked, but it was enough to show around the other two shops where the previous two victims had worked.

Whether anyone would remember the young waitress was something else entirely.

No one around Kaffee mit Schlag had remembered Heather ever acting strangely. None of the businesses, nor any of the panhandlers who passed through the area had any bad memories of her. She was always smiling. Always happy.

Disgruntled with her lack of success, Sara walked back to the alley where Ashley had been butchered and came to a stop.

A man and woman stood near the crime scene.

The male was older by at least ten years, and he looked worn and tired as he squatted down, his eyes seeming to devour the information the alley had to offer. Beside him, the younger woman had a predatory stance, one that said she knew how to handle herself in a fight, and that she wasn't one to back away from one.

Neither of them had the air of law enforcement, and they didn't have the appearance of journalists either.

They were different, and Sara didn't know if that was good or bad.

She watched them until the man straightened up and turned to speak to the woman.

When he did so, he spotted Sara and kept his mouth closed.

His companion glanced at Sara and smiled.

"Hello," the woman said, "how are you, detective?"

Sara bristled at the question and the fact that the stranger seemed to know her position. There was nothing on Sara that outwardly revealed her career choice, and the question surprised her.

"I'm fine," Sara said, walking up the alley towards them. "How can I help you two?"

"We don't need any help," the man said, giving her a small smile, "but thank you anyway."

"Let me rephrase that," Sara said, coming to a stop, five feet from them. "Why are you in the alley, and how did you know I was a detective?"

"We're in the alley," the woman said, "because we're investigating a murder. And I know you're a detective because you look like one."

"And what look is that?" Sara asked.

"The look of someone who knows what to look for," the man replied.

Sara raised an eyebrow. "Do you belong to an agency?"

The man shook his head.

"Nope," the woman said cheerfully. "We're just doing our own thing. You know how it is."

"I don't, actually," Sara said, her tone filled with ice. "I'd like to know your names."

"Victor Daniels," the man replied.

"Betty," the woman said with a wink. "Betty Crocker."

"How about a license, Betty?" Sara asked. She didn't like the young woman, and all she wanted was to find a reason to bring her in and put her in a holding cell for a few hours.

"Sure," Betty said. She took a man's wallet out of a back pocket, opened it and removed her license.

Sara accepted it and examined the identification. It had all of the appropriate stamps and marks, and the name on it was Elizabeth G. Crocker. 11 Drury Lane, Hollis, NH 03049.

"And I do know the muffin man," Betty said, winking again.

Trying not to grind her teeth, Sara handed the license back. "Get a lot of hassle as a kid?"

"Too much," Betty replied with an exaggerated sigh. "Kids always wanted me to bring baked goods to school. I can't bake to save my life. Can't cook either. Just frozen food and restaurants for me."

Sara realized she wanted to punch Betty, so she turned her attention to Victor, who had a look of frustration on his face as he looked at his companion.

"Have you seen this woman before?" Sara asked, handing him the photo of Heather.

Victor took it, studied it, and then shook his head. "No. I'm sorry."

"Have you?" she asked Betty.

The woman looked at the photo, all humor was gone from her face. Finally, she shook her head as well. "No. We will inform you immediately if we do."

Sara hesitated, unsure if the woman was joking again, but Betty wore a serious expression.

"Here," Sara said, removing a business card and handing it to Victor. "This is my direct line. Call it if you do see her."

"Will do, Detective," Victor said, pocketing the card and handing the photo back to Sara.

As she rolled the paper up and turned away, Betty spoke again.

"Detective," she said, and Sara heard cold, hard steel in the woman's voice.

"Yes?" Sara asked, glancing over her shoulder.

"When you find her," Betty said slowly, "she will more than likely have a ring on her finger. A class ring. Make sure you remove it and place it somewhere secure. Preferably a lead-lined box, if you have one."

"What?" Sara asked.

"Trust me," Betty said, her voice firm. "It would be best if you did so."

Surprised, Sara couldn't find her voice before the couple turned and walked away. And while Sara could have forced them to stop, she didn't.

Because, she realized, *I don't want to know.*

That small insight shook her, and it was in silent contemplation that she left the alley in search of some clue of the murderer.

***

"What was that garbage?" Victor hissed, his anger threatening to boil over.

Ariana glanced at him and grinned. "Oh relax, Victor. You need to lighten up. She would have taken us in if I wasn't an idiot."

"How do you figure that?" he demanded as they walked towards his hotel.

"Look," Ariana said, "she's a detective because she's smart. Which means she plays things close and the right way. She couldn't just haul us in without looking at our licenses, or at least one. I know you don't have a fake license, so your name would be completely credible."

"Betty Crocker?" Victor asked.

Ariana smiled. "Yup. Absurd, right? Sounds completely made up. Now, if the detective was to fly off the handle and drag us in after getting my name, but not an ID, then she would have looked like a complete idiot at the station. Granted, getting hauled in wouldn't have been fun, but it would have kept her away from us while we're investigating. And now, while we're probably not her favorite people, we showed we weren't worried about telling her who we were. Criminals don't do that. Well, stupid ones don't."

Victor shook his head, then asked, "When did you have a fake ID made?"

She laughed. "Victor, this isn't my first trip to New Hampshire. I have lots of fake IDs."

"Why in God's name do you need them?" he asked, confused.

A small smile flickered across her face and in a low, conspiratorial tone she said, "Because, Victor, I told you, I do things that I shouldn't."

She picked up the pace, and Victor let the matter drop, not wanting to know exactly what it was the young woman did.

CHAPTER 28:
HOME AGAIN, AND SAFE AGAIN

Stefan had pushed himself for the last two hundred miles of the ride back to his warehouse. He could have pulled over and rested on a back road. And he suspected he probably should have.

But he hadn't wanted to.

He was sore, and he wanted the relative peace and quiet that his minor fortress would provide. There was always the chance that Anne Le Morte would take the opportunity to launch an attack against him, but that was an event he had prepared for.

The unknown was what bothered him.

He felt certain he had gotten into and out of Concord, New Hampshire without being noticed. The only unknown was the long stretches of road between New Hampshire and Pennsylvania.

Others could have joined the hunt for him, seeking him out for the purpose of selling the information, or to bring him down.

Stefan didn't like either option.

So, instead of getting much-needed rest, he had pushed on. Black coffee, open windows, and loud music had helped for a short time, but not nearly long enough.

By the time he turned onto the stretch of road that lead to his warehouse, Stefan was having difficulty keeping his eye open. His wound had begun to throb, the pain pulsating rhythmically with the beating of his heart. He felt sick to his stomach when he pulled up to the gate, and his stomach only settled down when he found the locks were still secured and the salt intact.

Stefan knew he needed to patrol the perimeter, to see if there was any sort of break in the barriers.

Sleep, he told himself, driving back into the warehouse. *If you don't get some sleep first, you'll be open to an ambush. She'll kill you. Or her caretaker will. And whomever else she might have ensnared at this point.*

The paranoid part of him screamed for immediate reconnaissance, but the practical side won out.

He stumbled out of the car and locked it before he groped his way through the warehouse's semidarkness to his rooms. When he reached the door, he punched in the security code and then used his key. Two quick steps found him on the secure side of the door, locking it and enabling the alarm.

While his feet wanted to turn towards his small bed, Stefan forced himself to the observation room, and he brought up the security system.

He had installed new software before he had left for New Hampshire. The program, according to the company he purchased it from, guaranteed that it would record any event that the user configured as out of the ordinary.

Stefan considered any movement near the fence as out of the ordinary, and he had set the parameters accordingly.

And when he looked at the alerts, he saw there were no less than 49 of them.

A cold rage descended upon him and overwhelmed the exhaustion he felt. His fingers trembled as he typed in the password and accessed the files.

He watched as a dirty, unrecognizable figure carried a portable gasoline container up to the fence line. The stranger bent down and poured the contents out into a small spot, stood up and retreated toward the woods.

Stefan switched to the next alert and saw the process repeated in that camera. Again, and again the stranger poured the gasoline out until he or she had covered the entire perimeter of the fence. The stranger always avoided the front gate, where the strongest cameras were located.

Stefan watched the time stamp on each video, and fear joined the rage he felt.

Every thirty minutes, like clockwork, the stranger emptied a container.

And when the 49th one had spilled the last of its contents into the earth, the stranger threw the empty piece of plastic over the fence and walked away.

Stefan froze the image and enhanced it as best he could.

There was a small piece of paper taped to the container.

Stefan put on his body armor, snatched up his rifle, and hurried out of the room.

In a matter of minutes, he was at the part of the parking lot where the container lay, and he saw a piece of off-white paper taped to the battered red plastic.

Stefan counted to one hundred, then approached the container at an angle. He worked his way around it, slowly, keeping an eye out for any sort of trap. His gaze flickered from the red plastic to the tree line constantly, seeking any sort of hint that he was entering a trap.

When he felt satisfied that everything was fine, Stefan walked to the container.

He could smell the gasoline as he bent down to tear the paper free. Hastily, he unfolded it and read the three words written in block letters upon it.

I SEE YOU.

***

The shot sent her target sprawling back, the round slamming into his chest.

Grace Haussen watched as the man managed to get to his feet as she ejected one round and chambered another. She pulled the trigger a second time, but the weapon misfired. Angrily, she tried to remove the bad round from the chamber, but by the time she had done so, the man had vanished.

"Do not worry," Anne said in her soft, beautiful French, "we will have more shots at him. This will, in all fairness, work to our advantage. Fear is a powerful weapon, and he will be afraid every time he steps out his door."

"Yes, Miss," Grace said, shouldering the weapon after picking Anne up off the forest floor. "What now?"

"The hunter you killed," Anne said as they began to walk in deeper among the trees, "his flesh will not keep much longer. It would be best if you eat what you can, and then cook the rest. You will need your strength. Stefan Korzh is no meek kitten to tease and play with at our leisure."

Grace nodded her agreement. She remembered the sight of her mistress' previous protector, and the story Anne Le Morte told of a man named Bontoc who Korzh had killed.

All further concerns about the man her mistress hunted vanished beneath the dulcet tones of Anne Le Morte's voice, and Grace found herself skipping along the thin, narrow game trail towards their camp.

CHAPTER 29:
SWITCHING VEHICLES

Richard hummed to himself as he finished the last of the cuts, the young woman's flesh still warm beneath his hands. He wiped off a hand on his jeans, took a sip of water from the new woman's half-empty bottle, and considered his situation.

Heather, his fourth, and extremely satisfactory victim lay in the appropriate pose on the ground, and the arms of his newest acquisition, ached pleasantly from the struggle Heather had put up.

This is so rewarding, Richard thought, putting the knife away. He held his hand up to the light of the moon that pierced the high angles of the alley. The dark gem set within the silver ring twinkled and put a smile on his face.

It's good to switch bodies, Richard reminded himself. *Don't get comfortable in any one of them or else you might have a real problem staying free.*

The creak of old, unoiled hinges echoed off the bricks of the alley, and Richard jerked his head up.

A middle-aged woman stumbled out of a dull brown door, turned her back to him and became violently sick. The stench of vomit and cheap alcohol was carried on the wind, and Richard's smile widened.

***

Nicole Francine awoke with a pounding headache and her back screaming in agony. The night sky was directly above her, and it took her a moment to get her bearings.

Alley, Nicole thought. *You're in an alley.*

She gasped as she pulled herself into a sitting position, then clamped a hand over her mouth to both stifle a scream and to keep from vomiting.

A dead woman lay on the ground beside her, and when Nicole scrambled away, she saw that her hands were covered with blood.

Home! I need to get home! Oh my God, what happened? Did I see something and not remember? she thought desperately, clambering to her feet. *Is someone going to come back and do that to me? Oh my God!*

Go to the police, she thought, *that's all, just go to the police!*

Then a soft, whispering voice in her head stated, *They'll think I did it.*

They will, Nicole thought, panicking. *I was drunk. I don't remember what time I started drinking, or what time I left the bar. And what if no one saw me?! What if I don't have an alibi?!*

Unable to fight the fear any longer, Nicole ran for home.

CHAPTER 30

DISQUIETING INFORMATION

Detective Sara Milton stood in another alley, next to another crime scene.

Heather lay face up, her body poised as all the others had been. Her blouse was open, the perfect circle of stab wounds in the pale flesh. The left breast was cut open, revealing the pectoral muscle, and the section of it that was missing.

There was no fear in the dead girl's face. No hint that the event had caught her unaware.

What the hell is going on here? Sara asked herself, feeling sick to her stomach. *It's like the killings are a damned disease, an infection spreading from one victim to the next.*

How do I stop it?

She didn't have an answer.

Silently, she took a pack of gum out of her pocket, unwrapped a piece and put it in her mouth. She chewed slowly and stared at Heather's corpse, trying to think of what to do next.

***

Richard had allowed Nicole to consume half a bottle of wine after she arrived home, and then she had taken to hiding in some black abyss within her own head.

Richard didn't mind.

He enjoyed the feel of Nicole's body. The woman was in poor shape, physically, but she was more than a casual drinker. She needed alcohol to function, which made her an excellent vessel for travel.

Perhaps I might remain in her for two or three killings, he thought, *in spite of my own admonitions against it. It would be easy to have her remain drunk. She enjoys it so much.*

And in addition to that, Richard thought with a smirk, *I can see the crime scene right from her room.*

He stood in the window, looking down into the alley across the street while sipping on a bottle of wine. As the police and the investigators moved about the scene, Richard focused on an individual. A woman, sharp-faced and with an expression of determination on her face.

Ah, from the coffee shop, he thought, smiling. She had identified him, recognized him for the hunter he was.

And she is a hunter too, he told himself, turning away from the window and sitting down on the battered and sprung couch that was the apartment's sole piece of furniture.

Let the hunt begin, Richard thought and raised the bottle in silent salute to the woman who would seek to run him down.

***

Victor stood at the mouth of the alley, Detective Sara Milton's card in his hand. He was alone and waiting. Ariana had left after he had politely escorted her out of his room.

He hadn't heard from her since.

"Can I help you?" a large policeman asked, stepping over to Victor. The man's voice was polite but firm, and the set of his shoulders told Victor that no nonsense would be accepted.

"Yes, please," Victor said, smiling congenially. He handed the card to the officer and said, "I need to speak with Detective Milton about this case, if I could."

The officer, whose name badge read 'Junger', gave a nod and said, "Wait here."

Victor did as the man had bidden him to and watched as the officer walked up to the detective. She stood up, and the two of them spoke in a tone far too low for Victor to overhear anything.

When she looked in his direction, she nodded to the officer, took her card back, and walked with Junger to the mouth of the alley.

"Victor," the detective said with a tight smile, "what can I do for you?"

"I was wondering if we could speak in private for a moment," Victor said.

"Sure," Sara said. "Thanks, Gabe."

The officer nodded and went back to his post on the left side of the alley.

"Come on," Sara said, motioning to the building across the street. They crossed and came to stand in the small alcove of a closed and defunct florist. "What is it you would like to say?"

Victor had been up most of the night considering the answers to that question. And when she asked it, he gave her his best answer.

"Detective," he began, "the person committing these crimes might not be doing these intentionally. They might be under someone else's control."

Sara raised an eyebrow and asked, "And how's that?"

"Do you remember my colleague from the other day?" Victor asked.

"Betty?" Sara snorted. "Of course."

"She mentioned a ring," Victor continued, "and that you should look for it. It could be controlling the actions of the owner."

Victor observed her, a faraway expression slipping onto her face. After a moment of silence, the detective seemed to reach a decision.

"Victor," Sara said, "I have a body in the alley. The body of *another* young woman."

Victor winced, but he didn't interrupt her.

"This body," Sara continued, "is that of a woman named Heather. Up until I saw her corpse, I thought she was the killer. I thought that because I saw her enter an alley with another woman I assumed was the killer, only to find that first woman's body."

"My God," Victor murmured.

Sara nodded. "Now, you mentioned the ring. If we find the ring, will it stop?"

"That's what should happen," Victor stated. "But the ring has to be sealed up. It can't be let loose."

"I understand," Sara stated. "The problem is the ring then, and a ring is a hell of an easy item to hide."

Victor hesitated and looked at her, wondering, *Why is she accepting this so quickly? What does she know?*

Then he pushed the thought away and hated himself for the cynicism that had crept into his life.

"Yes," Victor agreed, "it certainly is."

"So as long as the ring is out there," Sara began.

"The killings won't stop," Victor finished.

Sara shook her head, spat on the ground and muttered, "Great."

The two of them stood in silence, watching the technicians work, and Victor suspected her thoughts ran along similar lines of his.

When is he going to kill again?

CHAPTER 31

FAR AND AWAY

Tom heard the stranger before he saw them.

A small, childlike creature crept through the shadows towards him, taking a long, cautious time to reach the cage.

When it did so, and could be seen in the pale moonlight, Tom saw that the creature was actually a man, though of slight build and short. The man's clothes were threadbare and patched in many places. His fingers were crooked and twisted, his feet swollen, and the toes gnarled. He was bent over, his head tilted up and cockeyed, looking at Tom through a pair of cloudy eyes that hid the color of the irises. His off-white, sickly and thin hair hung in loose, greasy strands.

He licked his lips nervously, revealing broken teeth and gaps where others should have been. His fingers twitched and spasmed as he looked at Tom.

"Hello," Tom whispered.

The man winced, then he offered a shy smile and whispered back in a broken voice, "Hello."

"My name is Tom," he said, presenting his good hand.

The stranger jerked back, hesitated, then reached out and gingerly took the offered hand.

"Silas," the man replied. He glanced around and asked, "Can you save me?"

The question caused Tom to shake his head in surprise, and Silas looked crushed.

"No, I didn't mean that I couldn't," Tom said hastily. "I'm just surprised. That's all."

"Oh," Silas whispered, his eyes wide and hopeful. "Can you?"

"Not from inside a cage," Tom replied. "I would need to escape, then find a way out of here. Do you know how we could leave?"

Silas nodded.

"And do you know how I could get out of this cage?" Tom felt his mouth go dry with anticipation.

"Yes," Silas whispered, and he produced a key from beneath his frayed shirt. "I stole the key."

Tom felt his heart rate quicken at the sight of a small, silver object in the man's hand.

Silas cast a furtive glance toward the shadows, then, with what seemed to be a great force of will, slid the key into the door's lock, and turned it gently to the right.

Tom held his breath, waiting for the inevitable click, and wondering how loud it would be in the curious stillness of the court.

Yet no sound was made.

Neither when the key turned, nor when the door swung open.

Tom took a deep breath, stepped out of the cage and felt a surge of strength rush through him as if his confinement had been draining the energy from him.

"Where did you come from, Silas?" Tom whispered once he was free.

"Albany, New York," Silas replied. "I was stolen from my home, a changeling left in my place. But something happened. The changeling died and I was never set free."

Tom cringed at the idea of it and Silas smiled sadly at him.

"Okay, how do we get out?" Tom kept his voice low, hardly more than a whisper, his eyes darting around and seeking out Cane, or anyone or anything that might come for them.

"This way," Silas whispered, and he hurried away, limping at a faster pace than Tom believed the man was capable of.

The man followed a slight, rock-strewn path that cut through thick ferns and low hanging branches heavy with Spanish moss. Every slight sound they made caused Tom to wince, but he focused on the back of

Silas, and soon they came into a small glade, the center of which was dominated by a large bramble patch. A hideous darkness clung to the plants, as if the shadows between the branches were deeper and fouler than any place Tom had ever seen.

"Quick," Silas said, panting, "we have to enter the patch. It is a door, from this world to our own, a way for us to leave. But I can only do it if you hold me. I've been here too long. I cannot leave on my own."

Tom nodded, went to pick the miniscule man up, and heard the rush of a heavy object coming towards him.

Instinctively, Tom ducked and twisted, seeing a large staff cut through the space he had vacated.

A tall, snarling creature was on the other end of the weapon, and Tom felt his stomach twist in revulsion. The beast stood on two legs and looked as if someone had torn his face off and then done a half-hearted job of sewing it back on.

The creature's skin was a mottled green, and he wore a dull brown tunic that covered his short and stocky frame. He reversed the staff, bringing it on a downward arc toward Tom, who dodged it as best he could, but the weapon clipped his prosthetic. The noise created by the contact of the two objects rang out through the woods, and in the distance, the sound of a hunting horn cut through the air.

Furious, Tom clenched his right hand into a fist and drove it up, smashing it into the creature's throat. He felt the larynx collapse, the windpipe follow, and heard the beast's last breath rush out of his pale lips.

The staff fell, forgotten, as the creature reached up and clawed at his own throat, desperate for air.

Around them, the sound of bodies crashing through the undergrowth rose up, and Tom twisted around, grabbed hold of Silas and pulled him close.

Without a word, Tom stepped into the bramble patch, and his stomach seemed to flip as the world shifted around him. Darkness folded around him and pulled him in deeper. Thorns pricked his clothes and sought out his flesh. Still Tom held onto Silas, and he pushed himself deeper into the bramble patch. Soon, dim sunlight replaced the otherworldly glow of the dark realm and air tainted by pollution assaulted his nose.

Tom's head spun, and his body seemed to gain weight as he staggered out the other side of the ring and into a dull, gray morning.

A quick glance around showed he was on a golf course, but he didn't know anything more than that.

He felt a shudder against his chest, and he looked down, remembering Silas.

Yet when he did so, Tom let out a gasp of surprise and dropped the man.

But there was nothing left.

Nothing living.

A withered, mummified carcass was all that remained. It was clad in the tattered clothes Silas had been wearing, and as Tom watched, the body disintegrated, leaving only the ancient fabric to flutter on a putting green.

Tom stared at it for a moment. Then the wind took the cloth and drove it against a sapling growing at the edge of the green.

A dull glitter caught Tom's eye; he crouched down, and he pushed aside some dust to extract a small crucifix made of silver. It was on a chain of small silver links, and Tom saw the name Silas Howe engraved on the back of the crucifix. The date 6 May 1939 was there as well, and Tom wondered how many decades Silas had spent as a prisoner.

"I'm sorry," Tom said, straightening up and slipping the necklace into his pocket. "I couldn't save you after all."

A cold fury began to build within him, and Tom walked slowly along the green, contemplating ways to destroy the world he had escaped.

***

Leanne stood at the bramble patch, the plants ignorant of what had transpired a short time before. The body of Makos lay on the ground; the goblin having suffocated to death from what looked like a blow to his throat.

"Elder," a voice said from behind her, "they are here."

"All of them?" she asked.

"Yes, Elder," came the answer.

Leanne turned around and faced the remaining human slaves. She counted eight in all and remembered the days when there would be a hundred or more in the woods, serving her every whim.

Leanne looked at the one who had spoken to her and saw a tall, dark elf dressed in the somber clothes of his tribe. His silver hair was pulled back in a loose ponytail, and he eyed her warily.

"Have you a knife?" she asked him.

He nodded and produced a long, slim blade.

"Kill them all and prepare a feast for me," she said. Glancing around, she spotted her daughter's husband. "I expect a dozen replacements for each by tomorrow. If not, I will feast upon your flesh."

Behind her came the first of the screams, and Leanne began the short walk back to her seat, mouthwatering in anticipation.

Chapter 32:
Sleepless

Stefan had taken to locking himself in his room during the few hours he slept each day. His chest, still bruised from the shot his body armor had absorbed, continued to ache and at times, he worried that he might need to make a trip to the hospital for x-rays.

He spent most of his time awake, fighting his growing anxiety and fear, and thinking of how to get rid of Anne Le Morte and her caretaker. Hours were spent in front of the computer, searching for ways to increase his defenses, and how to take back the initiative.

At one point, Stefan considered the option of hiring a company to clear all the land he had purchased. Yet that would have required the removal of the first caretaker's body, as well as the body of the hiker. And those acts would have left him dangerously exposed to Anne.

Stefan stumbled into his kitchen, dug a bag of ice out of the freezer, and placed it gingerly over his empty eye socket. At times, the pain was bearable. Those instances were few and far between, and the pain increased his anger, which caused his heart rate to spike, and his exhaustion to increase. It was a vicious circle that was bound to get him killed, either through some defect in his natural body or through a mistake made while he was too tired to think straight.

With the ice pressed firmly to his face, Stefan returned to his observation room. His eye flicked over the screens, searching for any sign of Anne's caretaker.

There was nothing.

The alert on his computer chimed, and he glanced down to see an order had arrived at the post office in Fox Cat Hollow for him. He tried to remember what it was he had paid for, but nothing came to mind.

Swearing, he logged into the account and then let out a laugh.

His listening equipment had arrived.

A feeling of relief swept over him, and Stefan stood.

Now, he thought, rubbing his chest and wincing at the pain, *I need to find a way to get to it without dying.*

***

Grace lay on the ground, Anne's slight weight a comfort against her back. The young woman had lost track of the days and nights she had spent with the doll. All she understood was that she never had enough time with Anne, and if the doll did not insist, Grace would never sleep.

The rifle was in front of her, the barrel smeared with dirt. Both she and the stock of the weapon were covered with cut brambles. She had lain there for two days, soiling herself and eating sparingly of the food she had gathered. Grace waited for Stefan Korzh to exit his warehouse, and when he did so, she would shoot him if she could.

Terrorize him if she could not.

A loud squeal pierced the gentle sounds of the forest, and when Grace looked, she saw one of the metal garage doors opening. She moved the rifle enough to sight down the barrel.

A moment later, a pickup truck pulled out. She watched it roll forward at a snail's pace, and she could see the driver look back at the garage door, waiting for it to slide back down into place and seal the building off once more.

Grace moved the barrel to follow the truck, and when it came to a stop at the exit, she prepared to shoot.

"No," Anne cooed. "No, not yet."

"Alright," Grace whispered, relaxing.

"I am not done playing with him yet. His fear is almost palpable," Anne said. "Do you understand?"

"Yes," Grace replied. "I understand."

"Good," Anne murmured, "then sleep, child, and we will kill Korzh when he returns. And should we fail, well, we will be in a fine position to finish the task at hand."

Grace nodded, closed her eyes, and obediently went to sleep.

CHAPTER 33

POOR PIERRE'S FINE WINES

Richard leaned against the bar, waiting for the bartender to fulfill his request for another glass of wine. He looked at himself in the mirror behind the bar and smirked, tickled to see Nicole's face respond to his commands. Idly, he played with his ring, twisting it around on his finger. He let his eyes move around the room by way of the mirror, seeking out any potential waitresses.

There weren't many to choose from, and none of them were particularly appealing.

At least not to his discerning palate.

He chuckled at the thought, and the bartender came over.

"How are you, Nicole?" the younger woman asked.

"Okay," Richard responded.

"That's a nice ring you have," the woman said, getting out a cheap bottle of wine and pouring it into a glass for Richard. "New boyfriend?"

He shook his head. "No. Just something I picked up."

"On your tab?" the bartender asked, nodding towards the wine.

"Please," Richard said, picking up the glass.

"Okay, just don't try and skip out tonight," the bartender reproached. "Bobbie's at the door, and he doesn't like it when you take off."

"Thanks," Richard said, and he glanced at the bouncer. He was a large man, bald and heavily tattooed.

A thumb in his eye and the fight will go out of him, Richard thought as he went and sat down in a booth. From within the wine-addled depths of Nicole's brain, he could hear the woman screaming, trying to fight him. Her fear was palatable, a distinctly sweet taste on the back of the tongue, and Richard enjoyed it tremendously.

He drank the wine fast enough to keep her drunk, but slow enough so that she still knew what was happening.

It's the little things that make life perfect, Richard told himself.

Over the next hour, he drank three more glasses of wine as he waited for the shift change with the waitresses. When it happened, he was sorely disappointed.

The new group of women was even less appealing than the first.

With a sigh, Richard stood up, walked unevenly to the bar, and paid the tab.

He made his way to the side exit, stepped out into the alley, and stopped to get his bearings.

***

Richard let out a snarl as he found himself suddenly incorporeal.

He heard a noise and shifted his position, his line of sight falling on the collapsed body of Nicole. Another woman stood above her, an aluminum bat in her hands. At her feet was a thin, emaciated man who was rapidly stripping Nicole of her valuables, including Richard's ring. The two assailants could have been twins, their faces gaunt and eyes sunk deep. Their skin was pale, and few teeth could be seen in their mouths.

Richard could sense a curious intoxication seeping out of them, and he knew they were under the influence of some narcotic.

"Is she dead?" the woman asked, glancing up and down the alley.

"Who cares?" the man snapped, digging Nicole's wallet out of her pocket.

Indeed, Richard thought, plunging into the thin frame of the woman. He seized control of her easily, raised the bat above his head and smashed it down on the skull of the male.

The bone crunched, and the blow jarred Richard's new arms up to the shoulders. But the man went limp and collapsed on the pavement.

Throwing aside the bat, Richard bent down, picked up Nicole's belongings, then robbed the man of his meager possessions.

Stepping over the two corpses, Richard hurried out of the alley and made his way to Nicole's dismal apartment. Once safely inside, he sat down, opened a bottle of wine, and slipped his ring onto his finger.

He spun it around, had a few drinks, and then smiled.

Moving from flesh to flesh, Richard thought, chuckling. *It is still for the best, no matter what hopes I had pinned upon Nicole.*

I'm sure of it.

CHAPTER 34:

NO REST FOR THE WICKED

Victor texted Tom, but there was no response. Finally, after nearly an hour of worry, he called Tom's cell. It went directly to voicemail.

"Tom, it's Victor," he said, "send me a text when you get this, please."

When he had ended the call, Victor thought about sending a text to Iris.

He might be with her, he told himself. *You know you would have been with your girlfriend if your parents were out of town. What teenage boy wouldn't be?*

Sighing, Victor put the phone down and resolved to try Tom again before he went to sleep, and not any sooner.

He went to the bathroom, started the shower, and undressed, and when he was ready to step in, someone knocked on the door.

Victor groaned, wrapped a towel around his waist, and went to the door, peering through the peephole into the hall. Detective Milton stood and waved at him.

"Unbelievable," Victor muttered, sliding the chain back and opening the door. "Detective."

She nodded, seemingly nonplussed by his state of undress, and asked, "May I come in?"

"Sure," he said, stepping aside. He closed and locked the door behind her.

"You want to take your shower?" the detective asked politely. "I can wait."

Victor started to say 'no', then he changed his mind. Chuckling, he nodded and said, "Yes. I'll be out in a minute."

"Sure," she said and went to sit down in one of the chairs.

Leaving her there, Victor walked into the bathroom and took a quick shower. Wearing a pair of loose-fitting pants and a t-shirt, he was still drying his hair when he stepped back into the room.

The detective grinned when she saw him.

"You weren't kidding," she said as he sat down across from her. "Most of the guys I work with, when they say they'll be out in a minute I know I can go eat lunch, play a quick game of cards and get back to my desk before they even think about finishing up."

"Not me," Victor said. "What can I do for you, Detective?"

"Call me Sara," she said. "I think we can skip any formalities."

"Sara it is," Victor agreed.

"Good." The humor on her face was replaced with a serious expression. "We've had two more deaths in an alley overnight."

"Same MO as the others?" he asked.

Sara shook her head. "No. Not at all. At first blush, it looks like a double homicide. We had a woman killed when she exited the bar. Blunt force trauma. Then, it looks as though the killer was murdered as he robbed the corpse. And he died of blunt force trauma as well."

"Okay," Victor said, rubbing at the stubble on his chin, "what makes you think it isn't a couple of guys with bad luck?"

"First is the dead woman," Sara said. "Nicole Francine. She was in a bar, drinking, which was her usual habit. But the bartender noticed that she was paying a lot of attention to the female wait staff. Not only that, but she said Nicole had a new ring on her finger. Big, old class ring the drunk said was from her new boyfriend."

Victor felt a foul taste in his mouth.

"And there was no ring on Nicole's body?" he asked.

"Exactly," Sara responded. "Which brings us to the dead man. He was part of what we called the Dynamic Duo. Danielle and Tyrell Smith. Brother and sister meth-heads. She was the muscle, he was the brains. Narcotics has picked them up more times than I want to think about, and they've never ratted each other out. You can't separate them. Or, I should say we couldn't."

"What happened?" Victor asked.

"We got a hold of some closed-circuit feeds from a store near the bar," Sara continued. "It shows the Smiths entering the alley. When we do a frame by frame, we could see Danielle had a softball bat under her sweatshirt. From the blows on Nicole's head and Tyrell's, we know she was the one who used the bat."

"Of course," Victor murmured. "Why did you bring it to me though?"

"Because," Sara answered, "no one else is going to listen to why she killed her brother."

Victor nodded. "Because I know she didn't kill her brother."

"Exactly," Sara declared. "You understand that whatever's in the ring has control."

Victor straightened up, surprised.

Sara offered a grim smile. "This isn't my first rodeo, Victor. Your friend's little comment about the ring. The killers becoming victims. And now, the Smiths. They all reminded me of some old cases I'd rather forget, but evidently, I'm not allowed to."

"You've dealt with possessed items before?" Victor asked, surprised.

"Two of them," she said, nodding. "And one ghost who kind of hung around an old factory. Enough to know that I don't like dealing with them. The man I used to go to, well, he died a few years ago and I sure as hell don't want to face off against this one in the ring on my own. I figured I'd come and talk to you since you seem to know what's going on."

"Yeah," Victor said softly, "I guess I do."

"I'm a detective, Victor," Sara said. "It's my job, and I'm good at it. I also know about you, and what happened down in Pepperell."

Victor stiffened and he looked at her in surprise.

"I had to check, to see if you were really who you said you were," Sara continued. "And you are. Victor Daniels, freelance writer and researcher. Recently widowed and residing in Fox Cat Hollow, Pennsylvania. As for your friend, Betty Crocker, she's as bland as bland can be, which makes me think she paid a lot of money to have it look that way. You're the real deal, though, and I appreciate that. Especially after your loss."

Victor took a deep breath, nodded, and then asked, "So, do you know where Danielle might be?"

"I have an idea," Sara replied. "Nicole, she was missing her apartment key. People I talked to said she always had it. She might lose her wallet, even her shoes, but never that key."

"Alright," Victor said, "you want to go to the apartment?"

"You're damned right I do," Sara answered.

"Okay then," Victor said, standing up, "let's go."

They left his room together, his phone forgotten on the table as the door clicked and locked shut behind them.

***

Ariana sat in her car, her keys in hand as she watched Victor exit the hotel in the company of the detective who had accosted them in the alley. She felt a vicious spike of jealousy stab through her, and she crushed it mercilessly.

Stupid, she snapped at herself. *Don't be stupid. He didn't even want me to stay the night. Look at his body language. There's nothing there. He has no interest in her. He doesn't have any interest in anyone other than his wife, and she's dead. I don't have a chance against that. No one does.*

The cold rationalization did nothing to prevent the burgeoning desire she felt for him from appearing again, and Ariana sighed. She sagged back in her seat and watched as Victor Daniels climbed into the passenger seat of the detective's vehicle.

Think, she told herself. *Think!*

She focused on the car as it backed up, straightened out, and then left the parking lot.

Starting her own vehicle up again, Ariana waited a moment before she followed them.

He left willingly, no sense of distress, she thought, forcing herself to review what she had seen. *I told her to keep an eye out for a ring. What if she's had experience before with the dead?*

Ariana grimaced at her own stupidity.

She hadn't checked the detective out, hadn't done any sort of research about the woman's history.

They're going after the ring, Ariana realized, and at the same time, she understood she couldn't follow them too closely. If she did, she risked giving herself away.

And why am I following them? she asked herself.

Ariana didn't answer the question because she already knew it.

Her feelings for Victor Daniels were as frustrating as they were undeniable, and she didn't want to see him come to harm.

Gripping the steering wheel, Ariana trailed them back into the center of the city.

CHAPTER 35:
GETTING HOME

Tom felt a shift in the air, a subtle scent that he couldn't identify but raised goosebumps along his arms, nonetheless.

He had come to a barn, the red paint on it faded, the equipment around it worn and battered from years of use. The dirt driveway was empty, and only a few chickens scratched around in the yard.

Tom stood behind the barn, having peeked around the corner at the dilapidated farmhouse. No one seemed to be home, and he was weighing the decision to commit a minor crime to get access to a phone. His legs ached, and his stomach let out an angry, rumbling protest at being empty for so long.

These concerns were forgotten as he felt the disturbance in the air. Keeping his back to the barn, Tom slid along the wall to the tall door that hung on a pair of rollers. Grasping the edge of the old wood, he let out a grunt, pushed the door out a little and slid into the cool depths. The stink of old manure and motor oil, the bitter sting of ammonia and the strangely soothing scent of hay all assaulted his nose.

He registered all of them as he let his eyes adjust to the dim light, then searched the interior for some object with which to defend himself. His eyes came to a stop on a pile of old tools stacked against the nearest wall.

No sooner had he reached it did he hear the rear door open.

Tom grasped the smooth, split wooden handle of an ancient and rusted hand scythe and dragged it out, shaking it free from the pile. He pressed himself into a shadow and watched Cane. What little light came into the barn did so from overhead, helping to hide him from her sight.

"Tom," she said, taking a step in, her nostrils flaring.

He remained silent, forcing his shoulders to relax while watching her move.

"You ran," she said.

She grinned as she looked around, taking a tentative step further in. "I'm here to take you back."

Tom continued to watch her, breathing slowly in and out of his nose.

"You're coming with me," Cane continued. "Either willingly or damaged. It does not matter to the Elder, so long as you are returned to her. She would have words with Victor Daniels, and I was on my way to him when she called me back. For you. She is displeased with your behavior."

Tom wanted to laugh, but the fear in his stomach kept him silent on that subject.

"You want to go home. I know. And you can do so after you have served your purpose," Cane said, stepping lightly to the right.

Tom shifted his position, saw her muscles tense, and he swung the scythe.

She sprang towards him with a speed he didn't believe possible. He barely had enough time to bring his prosthetic up, the hard composite serving as a small, but sturdy shield. The force of her slamming into him sent his body smashing into the wall, her jaws locking onto his false limb. The windows rattled in their frames, his teeth clattered, and stars exploded in front of him.

But he had buried the scythe in her belly, and he hadn't lost his grip upon the makeshift weapon.

A heartbeat later, Cane let go of his prosthetic and gasped, a sound made equally from surprise and pain. She tried to pull back, but Tom jerked the tool forward. The rough, dull blade of the scythe tore through her stomach and eviscerated her.

Snarling, Cane clamped a hand over his, not allowing him to remove the scythe even as her intestines spilled out onto the ground. With her free hand, she struck at him and Tom tried to twist away. She landed a glancing blow on his head which caused the world to tilt and spin.

Struggling to free himself, Tom drove a knee up into the inside of her thigh and he felt her leg shake as the muscle deadened for a moment.

With a shout of rage, Tom jerked his hand backward, wrenching the scythe out of her belly.

Her own hand remained clamped on his own and she howled as she smashed her free hand against his left ear.

The pain was instant and intense, causing him to dry heave as he staggered back a step. He couldn't hear anything from that ear, and he was afraid that she had ruptured the eardrum with the blow.

Cane stepped forward, screamed as she put her foot down in a loop of her own innards and slipped.

Tom twisted his right hand and pulled, freeing himself from her grasp and backing away from her, clutching the bloody scythe.

She stumbled back, her eyes wide and stunned, as if the pain had finally and fully registered. She pressed her hands against her stomach and looked down at the mess of intestines at her feet. For a brief moment she tried to pull them up and tuck them back in, but she shuddered and fell to her knees. She looked down at herself and let out a surprised laugh.

When her head lifted up, Tom could see the pain in her eyes and blood upon her muzzle.

"Finish it," she whispered.

Tom nodded, and without hesitating, he stepped up, raised the scythe above his head, and brought it crashing down onto her neck.

The cut wasn't clean, but it was enough.

Cane's lifeless form tumbled forward, jerking the blade out of his hand and leaving him shaking. With mute surprise, Tom watched as her body transformed itself from the curious hybrid of lupine and human into pure wolf.

She was once again the animal he had seen the first time outside of the house, a large creature both frightening and magnificent to behold, despite her being dead.

Tom stepped away from her as the front doors to the barn were torn open.

A trio of men stood in front of him, their angry demands silenced at the sight of him and Cane's body.

"My God, boy," one of the men said, "what the hell happened here?"

"A wolf," Tom managed to get out, then he watched the world fade from his eyes, and felt the earth rush towards him.

***

"You're awake," a voice said as Tom opened his eyes.

With a grunt, Tom pushed himself up and looked around. He was on a couch, an afghan over his lap, a glass of water on the coffee table next to him. For a moment, he could do nothing more than stare at the beads of condensation on the glass. He reached out, picked it up, and drank the entire contents in one go. His head throbbed and his ear ached, but he could hear in it.

Putting the glass back, Tom looked around for the speaker and found an older man who stood in the doorway of the room. He wore a sheriff's uniform of brown and khaki, a cowboy hat tilted back on his tanned forehead, and his arms crossed over his chest.

"Yes," Tom replied. "I'm awake."

He moved his shoulders and looked at the damage caused by Cane's teeth to the prosthetic.

Mostly cosmetic, he thought, propping the gouges with his fingers. *At least I won't need to get a new one.*

"You're lucky," the sheriff said. "Mighty lucky. That wolf should have taken your arm off."

Tom nodded in agreement.

"Where are you from?" the man asked.

Tom looked into the sheriff's deeply lined face and realized the man knew the answer to any question he might ask.

"Fox Cat Hollow," Tom answered.

"And your name?" the man asked.

"Jeremiah. Jeremiah Daniels," Tom lied, knowing that was the name on his falsified paperwork.

"You're a long way from Fox Cat Hollow, Pennsylvania, Jeremiah," the sheriff said evenly.

"Where am I?" Tom asked, and he could see the sheriff believed that he didn't know.

"Well," the man said, "you're just outside the city of Bridgeport, Jackson County Alabama, son."

Tom's hand shook, and he clenched it into a fist.

"Alabama?" Tom asked in a fierce whisper.

The sheriff nodded. "Know how you got here, son?"

"No," Tom said in a hushed voice. "Can't say I do."

"A pity," the man said with a genuine note of regret. "You have a fine friend up in Fox Cat Hollow, Pennsylvania. A young lady named Iris and her parents filed a missing person report this morning. I'm mighty interested in how you got down here from Pennsylvania in less than a day. Now, before you get all frantic and concerned, we were able to get a hold of the young lady, and your uncle, but not your father."

"My father's on a business trip," Tom said hoarsely. "Which uncle did you get a hold of?"

"Mr. Shane Ryan of New Hampshire," the sheriff replied. "He's wired some money to you for a flight home. We can help you get the arrangements, and he sent along enough for some fresh clothes, which is mighty fine. The ones you're in have certainly seen better days."

Tom glanced down at himself and realized his clothes were stiff with dried blood.

"Oh, the blanket," Tom moaned. "Did I ruin it?"

"No, son," the sheriff replied gently. "The Beauforts know how to get the blood out. Come on now, you've had enough excitement for one day, I think."

"Yeah," Tom said. "Yeah."

Then he dropped his chin to his chest and wept from exhaustion.

CHAPTER 36

LOOKING FOR A GOOD TIME

Joanne Kasacki winced as she walked out the kitchen entrance and into the bright sun of the morning. She stopped, sat down at the battered picnic table to the left, and pulled her sneakers and socks off. The cool air helped soothe her feet, which were aching and swollen from the double shift she had pulled.

From her purse, Joanne removed a pack of Parliaments, found her lighter, and lit a cigarette. It had been three hours since her last break, and her body was screaming for the nicotine. She inhaled, let the smoke curl around her lungs, then slip out through her lips as she parted them slightly.

Joanne sat in silence and smoked her cigarette down to the filter, then she stubbed it out and sighed.

Time to go home and get some sleep, she thought, wincing as she put her socks and sneakers back on. *At least try to get some sleep before the next shift.*

Joanne ground her teeth against the pain as she stood and walked gingerly towards the sidewalk. She followed the familiar path up the street, spotted her shortcut through the alley to home, and hesitated.

Word had been passed around by some of the third shift cops who took their lunch break at the restaurant, about a killer who targeted waitresses.

And they hadn't been joking, Joanne reminded herself. *Not that they ever joked about stuff like that. At least not with us.*

She didn't like the idea of taking the long way home, but she liked the thought of being dead even less.

Turning away from the mouth of the alley, she felt a sharp push in her lower back, and she jerked around.

A woman smiled at her, flashing a mouthful of rotten teeth.

Classic meth-mouth, Joanne thought, repressing a shudder. She forced herself to return the smile and asked, "You need something?"

"For you to go into the alley," the woman said, and it was then that Joanne saw the knife in the woman's hand. The weapon was flat black and deadly, held loosely and the woman gave every indication that she knew how to use the blade.

"Not happening," Joanne replied, her voice cold. "Put your little pig-sticker away and move along."

The woman sneered, raising an eyebrow and opening her mouth.

Whatever the meth-head was going to ask, Joanne didn't wait for it.

She drove her fist into the woman's sharp, narrow nose, and was satisfied to feel the cartilage break beneath the blow. Blood exploded from both nostrils as the woman took a shocked step back, and Joanne followed it up with two more punches to either side of the head. The pain in her feet was forgotten as she closed the distance between them, slapping the other woman's flailing knife-wielding hand away from her as she drove a fist into the woman's chest, narrowly missing the solar plexus.

The power behind Joanne's blow was enough to send the off-balanced woman into the wall. Again, the stranger tried to slash at her, and a second time Joanne blocked it, turning it aside easily as she drove a knee into the woman's thigh.

The stranger let out a wordless howl and escaped into the alley.

Joanne didn't chase after her.

In the close confines of the alley, the woman could easily turn the situation to her advantage and might also have a compatriot, which is what her Krav Maga instructor had warned her about.

Several people ran up to Joanne and asked her if she was alright.

Short of breath, all Joanne could do was nod, and when someone asked if they should call the police, she gave them a thumb's up.

Damn right, she thought and winced as she straightened up. *Call them, and let's see if that was the psycho hunting waitresses.*

***

Richard seethed as he fled up the alley, dodged down a narrow opening on the left and scrambled onto a dumpster. He used the dark green and rusted container to reach the lower rung of a fire-escape and pulled himself up, furious at the weakness of the body he had stolen.

Shut up! he screamed at the woman, the force of his thoughts sending her whimpering into some dark recess of her mind. His anger continued to rise as the arms and legs shook with exhaustion.

By the time he reached the first landing, Richard was gasping for breath. The sharp, biting sound of sirens told him he had no time to rest, and with a grimace, he pressed his face against the glass of the window that led to the fire-escape.

He saw an untidy kitchen beyond. Dishes piled high in the sink, trash over-flowing from the wastebasket. Taking his knife out, Richard jammed it up between the old wood of the sashes and managed to unlock them. He grabbed hold of the bottom sash, worked it free from the sill, and forced the window open.

The rank smell of bad chicken and old fish lashed at his nose, and Richard ignored them as he climbed into the apartment, his legs shaking.

He closed and relocked the window, then prowled through the small apartment.

Like the kitchen, the apartment was filthy, and it looked as though the resident was a bachelor. There were no photos of family, only a few various Irish Setters with a man who was shorter than the norm. In every picture, the man had a shotgun and was dressed in hunting attire.

Weapons, Richard thought, putting away his knife. *Are there weapons here?*

He refrained from opening any of the windows in the apartment, certain that such an act would attract someone's attention. And he knew he would be lucky if he hadn't already been noticed during his flight.

Richard returned to the kitchen, found a glass that was somewhat clean, and had several drinks of water.

The aches and pains of the fight began to make themselves known, as did the agony of his newly broken nose.

He shook his head in reluctant admiration.

I didn't know a woman could fight like that, he thought, sitting down. *She knew exactly what she was doing. I'm lucky to have gotten away. This is what you get for trying to move out of your standard operating procedure, fool. Stick to the drunks and the junkies. Don't try to play with anyone that isn't damaged.*

The idea of capture bothered him.

Had he been caught, they would have seized his, or rather Danielle's property, which included his ring. And his ring, he knew, would vanish into the depths of the police evidence room.

A place where Richard might be trapped for decades.

The thought was not appealing in the least.

I need another body, Richard thought. *One that won't threaten to collapse in a struggle, or seek flight from one.*

Danielle sobbed with relief when she heard him, and Richard smiled.

Don't worry, dear, he told her. Then, with a chuckle, he explained exactly what he was going to do to her when he shifted bodies again.

For a moment, Danielle was silent, processing what he had said.

Then her screams echoed within his own thoughts, and Richard grinned, wondering what body he might steal next, and what flavor Danielle's tainted flesh might hold.

CHAPTER 37

COMING TO A DIFFICULT DECISION

Stefan had driven to the post office in Fox Cat Hollow, picked up his packages, and returned to his home by a long and circuitous route.

From where he sat in the grass, shaded by the wide branches of a tall evergreen, he looked at his warehouse. He hated the lack of depth perception that had come with the loss of his eye. Beyond the tree line, he knew that Anne waited for him, and he knew her caretaker had a rifle. Whether there were any more rounds for it was unknown, but it was a question he didn't want to know the answer to.

The sun had nearly set, and he waited, hopeful that Anne's caretaker might be so foolish as to be revealed with the end of the day.

No luck, he thought, grumbling.

He waited until dusk had settled into place before he moved back towards the pickup truck. From the interior, he took out his keys and shouldered the backpack loaded with the equipment he had ordered. Finally, Stefan picked up his weapons, and prepared for a long, tense walk back. He would need to sneak onto his own property and reach the safety of the building without suffering any ill effects from Anne.

It was not an option he was pleased with.

With an angry sigh, Stefan readied himself and then began the laborious trip home.

***

Beneath the world of men, Leanne Le Monde dozed. The dark world had become somber and quiet with the loss of their slaves, and Leanne often smiled at the look of distress upon her kinfolk's faces.

They had not been saddened by the death of their servants. Rather, the fairies had been dismayed at the idea of having to work until they could steal more human children.

Let them sulk, Leanne thought lazily, pleased with the thought.

The sound of footsteps, loud and abrasive, reached her ears and Leanne opened her eyes a fraction of an inch to peer out at the loud intruder.

It was Guy, and the old wolf had a horrifying mask of hate stamped onto his face. In his left hand, he carried a large bag, in his right he held a rusted hand scythe.

Leanne stifled a yawn, stretched and sat up.

Guy came up to her, seething with rage. He offered a short, perfunctory bow, then straightened up.

"What news do you bring with such a scowl, Guy?" she asked languidly.

"I bring news of failure." Guy spat out each word as if he were clearing a foul taste from his mouth.

Leanne bristled at the tone in his voice but kept herself in check. He was one of the few who had earned the right to let the moderation of his words slip now and again.

"What news is this?" she asked. "And keep a civil tongue in your head now, Master Wolf, or I will have that tongue atop fresh bread."

He sneered at her, but his tone was modified nonetheless.

"The boy, Tom, has escaped Cane," Guy replied stiffly.

Anger caused Leanne's face to flush and become hot, and she bit back an angry reply. Once she composed herself, she asked, "And how did this happen?"

He threw the scythe on the ground in front of the dais, then he opened the bag and emptied its contents at his feet.

Cane's head rolled out, tongue lolling out between her teeth. Her eyes were a dull, milky white, and Leanne felt her stomach drop.

She sat in silence for a short time before she asked in a low, dangerous voice, "How did this happen?"

"The boy killed her," Guy answered.

"The boy?" Leanne demanded. "The skinny child held prisoner here? The thin invalid with only one of the two arms his God had given him?"

Guy gave a short, angry nod.

"Did he ambush her?" Leanne snapped the question at the old wolf, and he bared his teeth at her.

"No!" He spoke the word with such vehemence that it took Leanne by surprise. "There were spiders in the barn, and they saw the entire fight, short as it was. It should have been Cane, but there was no fear in the boy. He stood his ground, surprised her with a scythe. A rusted piece of metal claimed the best of my grandchildren!"

"Then seek revenge!" Leanne howled. "Go to the surface world, find him, tear out his heart and bring his corpse to me!"

A small, cruel smile appeared on Guy's face.

"I think not, Leanne," he said in a soft, cold voice. "I will mourn this grandchild, for I loved her dearly. But I'll tell you this; that boy won the battle, and when my granddaughter asked for the mercy blow, he gave it to her as best he could. I am thankful he gave her a warrior's death, and that it was enough."

"This is not an option, old Wolf," Leanne hissed. "You will hunt him down. You will do as I command."

"I will do nothing of the sort," Guy replied.

Leanne glared at him, raised her right hand, and clenched it into a fist.

The old wolf's neck crumpled like a piece of paper, and his eyes rolled up to reveal their whites. He hung limply in the air as if someone had threaded rope through his shoulders and suspended him from some unseen beam.

Leanne twisted her fist and listened with satisfaction as Guy's neck snapped, his head turning around until she was looking at the back of it. She shook her hand, and his body replied in kind. With a snort, she opened her fist, and his body collapsed to the ground.

Reclining into her chair, Leanne looked at the corpse and smiled. She had forgotten how greatly her powers were amplified in her homeland, and how much she had missed it. Still smiling, she considered what step to take next.

CHAPTER 38

NOT NEARLY FAST ENOUGH

Tom fought the exhaustion that threatened to overwhelm him in the hot interrogation room. The sheriff had brought Tom to the station to 'talk' to him about how he had gotten from Pennsylvania down to Alabama. And Tom had given him an answer, albeit one with a significant amount of the truth missing.

The sheriff, unfortunately for Tom, wasn't a fool.

Shifting in his seat, Tom rubbed at his eyes with his hand, and then looked at the door when it opened. The sheriff, with an expression of sincere displeasure, walked into the room and sat down at the table, across from Tom. A few minutes earlier the man had stated he would fetch something for each of them to drink.

His hands were empty, and Tom fought the urge to ask where the beverages were. He could sense the sheriff was in no mood for any sort of sarcasm, and that should he push his luck, Tom might well end up in jail for the evening.

Or longer, Tom thought. While Victor had paid a significant amount of money to help Tom disappear from Connecticut, there was always the off chance that something could happen.

"Jeremiah," the sheriff said, his jaw firm and his eyes steady, "tell me how you got down to Alabama."

"I don't know," Tom lied. "I left my house, that's the last thing I remember. Then, a little while ago, I woke up in a field and went looking for help. I found the barn, and that dog attacked me."

"Wasn't a dog, Jeremiah," the sheriff stated. "Biggest damned wolf I've ever seen or heard of."

"I don't think it matters," Tom replied. He held up his prosthetic and pointed at the deep bite marks. "This is important. If I wasn't already missing an arm, then I definitely would have been after she got her teeth into me."

"How'd you know it was a she?" the man asked lightly.

Tom felt his face redden as he shrugged. "Just a guess. Had a fifty-fifty chance, right?"

The sheriff nodded, tapped on the table lightly and asked, "You have a curious accent, Jeremiah."

Tom raised an eyebrow but didn't respond.

The sheriff tilted his head, saying, "Now, I've met people from Pennsylvania before, and they don't quite sound the way you do. New Englanders though, hmm, yes, you've got that accent. It's like someone's pinching your nose together every time you speak."

"Funny," Tom said, "no one's ever told me that before."

The sheriff continued to speak as if Tom hadn't said anything at all. "In fact, if I was to pinpoint a New England state, I'd say you sound like you come from Connecticut. Somewhere in the southeastern corner. Down near the coast."

Tom felt a chill spread through him, accompanied by a wave of helplessness. The man across from him wasn't a ghost to be trapped or destroyed. He wasn't a madman to escape from, or a werewolf to disembowel.

The man was a sheriff, an officer of the law, and he had the ability to send him back to Connecticut, into the hands of the asylum.

Beneath the edge of the table, Tom gripped his prosthetic hand to keep the other from shaking.

"Have you ever been to Connecticut before, Jeremiah?" the sheriff asked in a low, relaxed drawl.

"Can't say that I have," Tom answered. "I'm from Massachusetts, originally. Pepperell. Me and my dad, Victor."

"Adoptive father?" the sheriff asked.

Tom almost nodded, but he shook his head instead. "No. My mom died about a year ago."

The sheriff tapped his fingers on the table again. "That so? I'm sorry to hear it. Strange, you know, not having any other folk to call for you. Just your dad."

"And my uncle, and my girlfriend," Tom retorted, keeping his voice under control. "I'd like to call her, by the way. Let her know I'm okay."

"Hm, we'll see. And the girlfriend doesn't count when it comes to getting in touch with someone," the sheriff said easily, sitting back in his chair. "No. Not by half. Put a ring on it, boy, then she'll count. But I'd put my money on Connecticut. Hell, I'd put a lot of money on it. In fact, now you're not going to believe this, but your prints came up as a match for a kid missing out of Connecticut. Strange, isn't it?"

"It is," Tom agreed, surprised at how steady his voice was. "What's stranger is that you didn't fingerprint me, and since I've never been to Connecticut, I can't see how I would have been fingerprinted there."

The sheriff gave him a small smile. "True, we didn't fingerprint you. Silly of me. Thought we had. You know, it's usually the way it goes when I have someone in here."

Tom nodded and waited.

"Now," the sheriff continued, "we were going to let you have the money to purchase the ticket back to Pennsylvania, but since you popped up as a possible match on the National Center for Missing and Exploited Children, that's not going to happen."

"It's not?" Tom asked, anger beginning to replace his caution.

The sheriff shook his head. "No. We're going to put you in a foster home until Connecticut can send someone down here to help us figure this out."

Tom stared at the man, and the sheriff's face paled slightly beneath his tan. The smug expression that had appeared on the man's face vanished and a mixed look of anger and concern replaced it.

"Son, don't you look at me like that," the sheriff snapped.

"I'll look at you any damned way I want," Tom snarled, his fear forgotten. "My girlfriend reported me missing. My god-damned uncle sent you money to get me home, and you've got the audacity to hold me here? And why? Because I look like some kid in Connecticut? What'd this kid do, take off running for someplace?"

"Son," the sheriff said again.

"I'm not your son!" Tom yelled. "My father's on a business trip, my mother's brother wants me home, and you're holding me here!"

The sheriff straightened up, his face darkening with anger.

"Tell me this," Tom hissed, undoing the straps on his prosthetic, "the kid in Connecticut, he was missing an arm, too?"

He slammed the limb down on the table, shaking it. The damaged prosthetic lay between them, and the sheriff's face paled again, and Tom knew he had him.

"Yeah," Tom growled, "I didn't think so."

"How long—" the sheriff started.

"Stop," Tom said, interrupting him. "I want a few things right now, Sheriff. Either the money to get my damned ticket to go home, or a representative from whatever passes for youth services in Alabama. Because if I'm going to stay here any longer, it's going to be with a representative, a lawyer, and a camera to record everything that goes on."

Without a word, the sheriff got to his feet and left the room, slamming the door behind him.

Shaking, Tom picked up his prosthetic and started to strap it on when he heard a commotion outside of the interrogation room's door.

Twisting in his chair, Tom heard a stream of profanity, a raised voice, and then a familiar one.

"I don't give a damn, Sheriff," Shane Ryan said, "you're going to give me my nephew!"

The sheriff's response was unintelligible, but Shane's was clear and crisp.

"Listen to me, Sheriff," Shane said, and there was a deadly quality to the man's voice. "I served in the Marines for over twenty years, and one thing I learned about the South is that they respect those of us who served. How well do you think it's going to sit with the rest of the folks here when they learn you refused to help me?"

"Sir," the sheriff began.

"Sheriff," Shane said, "either you're going to open that door, or I'm going to open it. You choose."

The doorknob twisted and the sheriff stepped aside, his face red and his expression one of pure fury.

"Hey kid," Shane said, striding into the room. "You okay?"

Tom could only nod. After a moment, he was able to say, "I need to call my girlfriend. She's got to be worried sick about me."

"Here," Shane said, handing him his cellphone.

Wordlessly, Tom accepted the phone, and with a trembling hand he dialed Iris' number.

CHAPTER 39

AT THE APARTMENT

They stood in the hallway of Nicole Francine's apartment.

If the meth-head was hiding in the apartment and had the ring on, they were going to be in for a fight, and a difficult one at that.

"Do you have a key?" Victor asked, his voice low.

The detective shook her head and said softly, "No. We haven't been able to get over here. Since Nicole wasn't butchered like the others and since we know it was Danielle who killed her, this investigation's on the backburner. We have patrolmen keeping an eye out for Danielle, but that's it."

"Great," Victor muttered.

"Ready?" Sara asked.

Victor nodded and she knocked on the door with an authority reserved for police officers and Marines, and when no one responded, she knocked again. After the second time, Sara leaned forward, pressing her ear against the battered wood of the door.

Victor watched as the woman frowned, straightened up, and banged on the wood one more time.

The only sound Victor heard was that of coughing from another apartment.

Sara shook her head.

"Either she's not answering," the detective said, turning away from the apartment, "or she's out somewhere."

"I don't think either one's a good option," Victor said.

"They're not," Sara said, leading the way down the hall toward the stairs. Within a few minutes they were back on the sidewalk, and Sara's phone rang.

"Hold on," she said and stepped away to answer it.

Victor looked in the other direction, wondering where the killer might be.

Who he might be is a better question, Victor thought. *He's jumping from body to body, and if we don't get a line on him soon, we're going to end up with more victims.*

"Hey," Sara said.

Victor turned to face her. "What's going on?"

"There's been another attack," Sara said.

"Another body?" he asked, unable to keep the sadness out of his voice.

Sara flashed him an exuberant grin as she shook her head. "This victim survived the attack. Description of the assailant matches Danielle. Listen, I'm going to drop you back off at your hotel. I've got to get over to the hospital to question the victim."

"Go ahead," Victor said, waving the woman on. "I'll call for an Uber or Lyft."

He reached for his phone, patted his pockets, and let out a snort of disgust.

"What is it?" Sara asked.

"Seems like I left my phone back at the hotel," Victor said, shaking his head.

"So, do you want that ride?" The detective glanced at her watch.

"No," Victor said, smiling. "I can find my own way back. And it's nice out. Walking will do me good."

"Are you sure?" Sara asked, and Victor could see that while she was concerned, she also wanted him to be fine.

"I'm sure," Victor said, nodding. "Let me know what you find."

"Yeah, I will," Sara said. Without a backward glance, she hurried to her car. In a few moments, she pulled away from the curb, and Victor was alone on the sidewalk.

He slipped his hands into his pockets and started along the street.

***

Richard had found a bottle of cooking sherry in the apartment he had broken into, and while it had a nasty, foul taste to it, the liquor was enough to keep Danielle quiet.

Shivering against the cold and hating the weakness of the woman's body, Richard walked hunched over as quickly as he could. He had a vague notion of where Nicole Francine's apartment was, and once he got back to it, he could focus on acquiring another body. With the present frailty of Danielle's body, he couldn't risk another attack.

The last woman had been far too strong. Too skilled in attack and defense, and it had nearly cost him.

He turned onto a small street and realized that the area seemed familiar.

Richard paused, took stock of his situation, and a block up the street he recognized the bar Nicole had been drinking in prior to her murder.

Letting out a sigh of relief, Richard hurried towards it, whistling as he went.

***

Victor stepped out of a corner store, a newspaper folded under his arm, a power-bar in one hand, and a bottle of water in the other. He moved to the left of the door, opened the water, and took a drink.

At a street corner, he spotted a thin, young woman with a haggard appearance, and slowly lowered the bottle. His eyes never left her as she glanced from one side to the other, then walked towards the apartment building he and the detective had left only a few minutes before. As the thin woman drew closer, Victor saw a large, silver ring on her index finger.

Slowly, Victor put the cap back on the bottle, opened his power-bar, and watched the woman from the corner of his vision.

Without looking back, she opened the foyer door for Nicole's apartment building and stepped into its depths.

Victor took a bite of the bar, turned toward the building, and felt a hand on his arm, restraining him.

He jerked his head to look at the owner of the hand and wasn't entirely surprised to see Ariana.

She shook her head.

"No," she said in a low voice. "You don't have any sort of protection with you, and whoever's in that ring, they're not to be trifled with. None of them are. I think you've learned that by now, Victor."

The way she spoke his name shook him.

She did it with the same care and affection he had heard from Erin.

Unable to speak, Victor could only nod.

"Come on," she said. "My car's over here. We'll sit down and figure out what the best move will be."

Victor allowed Ariana to lead him away, wondering how he and Ivan Denisovich's daughter were working together.

CHAPTER 40:
A NEW EFFORT

Stefan had made it into his home without being fired upon.

Still vigilant, he crept through the warehouse in his bare feet, holding his shoes in his left hand. The straps of his backpack cut into his shoulders, the weight of the sound equipment pressing down upon them. By the time he made it to his small quarters, he was fairly certain he was alone.

Once inside, he knew it.

He let out a sigh of relief and was instantly disgusted with himself.

People should be in fear of me, he thought angrily, heading into the room where he kept some of the more controllable possessed items.

They were arranged on a five-tier metal shelf, each object labeled with the name and habits of the deceased attached to them. Some were mean-spirited and caused mischief. Others enjoyed torturing the living. Only three were killers. Killers who were entirely open to suggestions.

Stefan stared at the shelf for several minutes, thinking. When he finished, he nodded and took down one item. A black, hard plastic comb in a hand-tooled, brown leather case.

The object was uncomfortably cold in his hands as he carried it into the kitchen and set it down on the table. He sat down and said, "Come out."

The chill in the room deepened, and he ignored it, refusing to succumb to the cold attempting to seep into his bones.

A young man appeared, his black hair curled up in a wave away from his forehead, the sides slicked back. He wore a plain white t-shirt, the sleeves rolled up and a pack of cigarettes tucked into the left sleeve. His jeans were rolled as well, the pale cuffs barely touching the black

Wellington engineer's boots he wore.

The young man looked at Stefan, glanced around and asked, "Where's your, Ma, kid?"

"She's dead, Bucky," Stefan answered.

"She didn't hang around after?" the dead man asked with genuine surprise.

"No," Stefan stated dryly, "which makes me believe there may be a God after all."

Bucky snickered. "No such luck, kid. Leastways, not for me. What's the deal? Why am I here?"

"I have a problem," Stefan replied. "I would like you to take care of it."

"Really?" Bucky asked, taking his cigarettes out and lighting one.

Stefan hid his fascination with the act, impressed by how the dead managed to do tasks in death that they had once done in life.

"And what do I get out of it?" the dead man asked.

Stefan wanted to threaten him, to demand his cooperation, but with Bucky, a different approach was needed.

"You like to scare people more than you enjoy killing them," Stefan stated.

Bucky nodded.

"There is a large stadium nearby," Stefan continued. "Hundreds of thousands of people pass through there each year. I can hide your comb somewhere in the structure. You would have the entire facility to roam. Countless individuals to terrify."

A hungry look appeared in the dead man's eyes, and he exhaled a cloud of ghostly smoke toward the ceiling.

"Lots of people?" Bucky asked, greed thick in his voice.

"More than you can possibly imagine," Stefan said. "You would have your pick every day."

Bucky chuckled and asked, "So, what's this problem you need taken care of?"

"Someone is in the forest here, with one of my parents'

possessions," Stefan explained. "I would like you to go into the woods and relieve the caretaker of their life."

Bucky raised an eyebrow and asked, "Kill them?"

Stefan nodded.

"And this is something you can't do?" Bucky asked, his lips twitching with a smile. "Is that why you have an eye-patch there, Captain Hook?"

Stefan ground his teeth, forced himself to smile and said, "I lost an eye, not a hand. But the man who took it still lies in the forest, his body rotting. And as for the caretaker, I cannot risk going in with such a handicap. At least not yet."

"So, there's a rush on this?" Bucky inquired.

"There is," Stefan said. "The sooner you kill the caretaker, the sooner I will get you into the stadium."

Bucky grinned. "Sure. I'll take care of it. They close by?"

"Within a mile, at least," Stefan said.

"I'll take care of it," Bucky said, nodding. "Get your wheels ready, because I want to go as soon as it's done."

Stefan picked his keys up from off the table and rattled them at the dead man.

With a chuckle Bucky disappeared, taking the chill of the grave with him.

A wave of calm washed over Stefan as he stood up and went to the cabinet. He took down his vodka, poured a glass, and carried it with him to the observation room.

I hope they're close enough to be seen, he thought, sitting down in his chair and glancing at each monitor. *I would surely like to watch them die.*

CHAPTER 41

A DISRUPTION AND A LESSON

Grace no longer worried about hygiene, or whether she might have enough money to go out with her friends. Occasionally, flashes of her life before Anne Le Morte interrupted her thoughts, but those were becoming rarer.

Life with Anne was perfect. Grace protected the doll, and the doll cared for her needs. When Grace was hungry, Anne helped her find food. When she was thirsty, Anne found her drinks.

The weather was warm, and the small shelter the caretaker before her had created was more than sufficient for her needs. She had lined the interior with pine boughs, covered with clothes she had salvaged, and from the two men and the others she had slain deep in the woods.

Her thoughts were occupied with only one concern, the protection of Anne Le Morte.

Grace's head jerked up when she caught movement out of the corner of her eye, and for a moment, a shard of fear pierced her. Panic joined, and she felt certain she had failed Anne, that someone had snuck up to their small home and was prepared to take the doll from Grace.

Yet nothing of the sort happened.

Am I hallucinating? she asked herself, staring at the man across from her.

He was young and disturbingly translucent, more of an afterthought, or perhaps a memory of some film she had seen. The stranger didn't look as if he belonged in the modern world, and he reminded her of Marlon Brando in *The Wild One*.

Grace blinked several times, but when the young man remained, she shrugged and went back to her meager meal of salvaged food and dried, human flesh.

The stranger approached on silent feet, the underbrush passing through him as he moved. When he finally came to a stop a short distance from her, Grace looked up at him again.

"Go away," she said, gesturing with her free hand. "I don't have time for you."

The young man scoffed, squatted down, and looked at her with a small smile.

"You don't have time for me?" he asked, his voice low and pleasant.

Grace shook her head. "I'm hungry. Once I'm done eating, you'll go away. They always do."

He smirked and seemed about to speak again when the doll moved beside Grace.

Anne Le Morte turned her head to look at the stranger.

"Who are you?" the doll asked in French.

The stranger glanced at the doll and asked Grace, "What'd she say?"

"She wants to know who you are," Grace answered, sitting back. In French, she asked, "Anne, what do I do about him?"

"Nothing," Anne replied in with a purr, "he is my kind, my dear Grace. You will translate for me?"

"Of course," Grace answered.

"Tell him who I am," Anne said.

Grace did so, and the stranger laughed.

"Well, that's just a little bit of fantastic," the young man said. "I'm here to see her, and to take care of her. And to kill you, too."

Grace told Anne what the man said, and then took a bite of her food.

As the man straightened up, he came to a sudden stop, a pained expression settled on his face. Grace chewed methodically as he tried to twist to the left, then to the right. She watched him struggle to move any part of himself and was pleased to see he could not.

"What's going on?" he demanded.

Grace translated as Anne spoke.

"I can only assume," the doll said, "that Stefan Korzh has promised you something he cannot deliver. And I must assume that this prize he has offered you comes at the price of myself and my protector. Unfortunately for you, you shall not succeed here today. Nor any other day for that matter."

The young man opened his mouth to protest, and his lips were pulled together, large, rough twine threading through his lips. Grace watched as his shirt was stripped from him by unseen hands, and large stitches joined the flesh of his arms to that of his chest and stomach. Within moments his jeans were torn away, and the process was repeated.

He howled through his sewn lips, his eyes filled with a mixture of pain and fear.

"Is it not wonderful, my beloved Grace, to see what I can do against one of my own?" Anne asked.

Grace nodded, and as she did so, she saw the dead man's scalp slowly peeled back from his forehead.

She watched for a moment longer, then rummaged around the camp, looking for something to drink while Anne went about her business.

⁕⁕⁕

The comb lay in its case on the desk as Stefan watched the monitors in the observation room. Occasionally, he glanced at the possessed item, wondering when Bucky would return and inform him of the situation.

A sharp, sulfur stench filled the air, and Stefan looked around, his eyes coming to rest on the comb.

With a growing sense of horror and despair, he watched a small, tight, and bright blue flame spark into life at the comb's center. The fire danced along the item, devouring it.

Within seconds, nothing remained except for a slight pile of smoldering ash.

Bucky was dead, and the only information gained was unpleasant.

Anne was stronger than he thought, and she controlled the world beyond the compound.

I'm going to have to hunt her, Stefan thought bitterly.

Sighing, he took out a pen and paper and began to write down what he would need to do if he had any hope of surviving.

CHAPTER 42:
DISAPPOINTMENT AND DISARRAY

Leanne lay on her bed, staring at a sky she hadn't seen in two hundred years.

The stars that hung above the dark world were different than those that shined above humanity.

After her daughter's death, Leanne had gone into a self-imposed exile, and she had nearly forgotten the joys of her own world. The death of Jean Luc, who had been her sole companion and a pleasant reminder of home, had served as the impetus for her return.

And since her arrival and reclamation of the position of power, Leanne had been unable to enjoy the simple pleasure of gazing upon the stars.

There hadn't been any time.

With Tom's escape, Cane's death, and the unfortunate need to execute Guy, she needed some time alone to gather her thoughts. To focus on what had to be done next.

Victor Daniels must still be brought to me, she thought angrily. *He must answer for his part in the death of Jean Luc. It matters not that he bears no responsibility for it, our laws are old, and he must not escape our judgment.*

She smiled at the thought.

With her return to her homeland, she had begun to shed the alien norms and ideals of the humans with whom she had related for so long.

It feels right, she told herself, *to be home. All is as it should be. Except for Rowan.*

The thought of her daughter, dead, caused her smile to fade away. She could remember when Rowan had taken her place upon the dais, the joy of that day. But the memory of her death followed close upon the heels of the first.

Leanne had torn into the ranks of fairies and men alike, seeking out some sort of answer. Any answer.

But there was nothing to be found.

Not a clue.

One day, Leanne thought bitterly, *one day I will know who killed her, and I will burn the world to its core if I must, in order to have my vengeance.*

A soft whisper cut off further thoughts, and Leanne straightened up, eyes darting around the small courtyard that served as her bed chamber.

Rustling arose from the thick hedges, and the gentle creak of the door set into a pair of granite posts caught her ear.

Leanne stood up, fingers curling and relaxing as she sought out the source of the noise. A smile played across her face and anticipation built up within her.

Come out, she thought. *Come and see me. I'll know who it is who hunts me here, in my own domain. Where is your courage?*

There was a sigh behind her and Leanne twisted around, bringing her hands up to strike, but it was too late. Her attackers were already there. Strong hands grasped her arms and kept them pinned to her side. A gag was stuffed into her mouth, and a hood dropped over her head, a cord binding it tightly around her neck.

She struggled against them, desperate for breath, and some struck her in the face, knocking her to her knees.

Then Leanne recognized the voice of the man she had usurped.

"Bring her," he said in a melancholy tone. "We will put her in the ground beside her child."

Leanne howled and fought against her captors.

But it was useless. She could neither breathe nor stand, and with a deep, shuddering fear she knew she would be buried alive.

CHAPTER 43

GOING IN AND GOING HARD

"What do you have here?" Victor asked Ariana, not taking his eyes off the front door to the apartment building.

"Not much, I'm afraid," Ariana replied. "I wasn't planning on doing this today. I had hoped to get to it this evening, and that would have left me time to get back to my own hotel room."

"Okay," Victor said, risking a quick glance at the younger woman. "Then what do you have?"

"Gloves," she answered, "and a hammer."

"Gloves and a hammer," Victor repeated. Then he looked at her, forgetting about the building. "A hammer? My hammer?"

Surprisingly, a slight blush rose to her cheeks.

"Yes," she said, focusing on the apartment building, "your hammer."

"I thought it was lost when the house was destroyed," Victor said, returning his attention to the building. "You could have given it back."

"Could have," Ariana agreed. "Obviously, I didn't. No use crying over spilled milk."

"No use at all, evidently," he snapped. "Can I have it back when we're done?"

"Depends," Ariana said.

"On what?"

"On whether or not we make it out," she said in a hard tone. Do you understand?"

"Yes," he answered, looking over his shoulder.

"I'm serious. This ghost, he's worse than the others," she said. "You need to remember this. He's different. He literally will not hesitate to eat us alive."

"They're all bad," Victor retorted and got out of the car.

Ariana followed a moment later, opening the trunk of the vehicle and extracting two pairs of white gloves and the hammer from a Target shopping bag. Wordlessly, she handed him the hammer and a pair of gloves. Victor put them on, grasped the familiar, comforting weight of the tool and nodded to her.

They were silent as they crossed the street, reached the building, and went inside.

**

Richard sat on the counter, swinging Danielle's thin legs and contemplating the next place he would go to kill someone. The world was open to him, and the idea made him smile.

There are enough junkies and drunks for me to travel across the world, he thought. *I can sample flesh on every continent, from every culture. And if I am caught, what can they do? They can't kill me.*

The idea of it caused him to snicker, and he jumped down to the floor. Nicole's apartment was safe and secure for the moment, but it would be too dangerous to remain there much longer. Danielle was obviously not the attractive waitress, and the police would eventually arrive to search the rooms to see if there was any hint as to why Nicole had been killed. They might even discover she had killed someone as well, and they would wonder why.

And they will know nothing, he thought, grinning. *Which is as it should be. Putrid little fiends.*

He passed by the door to the apartment and stopped.

A creak had sounded in the hall as if someone was attempting to remain quiet and unheard.

Richard reached down into his pocket, drew out the black folding knife and opened the blade. Taking long, deep breaths, he watched the door and waited.

***

Victor watched as Ariana held up three fingers. Then she counted down silently, and when she reached one, she kicked open the door.

"Hello," Danielle said in a rough, broken voice, and she drove the blade of a knife into the side of her own throat and ripped it out the front.

Blood sprayed out in a fountain, the thin young woman remaining on her feet for only a moment before collapsing to the floor of the apartment.

Both Victor and Ariana stood there for a split second, then an unseen force slammed into Victor's back, sending him hurtling into the apartment. He slipped in the blood, tripped over the fresh corpse, and fell on both knees. The impact sent bolts of pain shooting up through his thighs, his teeth slamming into one another. A heartbeat later, he was knocked onto his face as Ariana was thrown into him.

As the door slammed shut, Victor twisted around and saw the ghost of a young man. He was dressed in military fatigues, and his neck had a vivid red mark around it.

The dead man grinned at Victor and said, "Let's play, shall we?"

Before Victor could reply, the ghost struck him again. The blow was cold, brutal, and calculated. It struck Victor on the left ear, pain exploding in his eardrum and leaving his head ringing. He tried to scramble out from under Ariana, who had been knocked out and searched for the hammer which had flown from his hand.

Victor spotted it, reached out for the hammer, and screamed as the ghost kicked him in the face. The strike was vicious, leaving his lips cold and numb and spots flashing in front of his eyes.

"I'm curious," the dead man said. "How did you find me? You don't look like police. There isn't that sense of bumbling efficiency about you. No, the two of you seem as if you know a thing or two about the dead."

"A thing or two," Victor gasped, pulling himself away and further into the apartment. "I know you're a murderer."

The dead man grinned and lashed out with a boot, the toe of which caught Victor in the thigh, deadening the muscle and eliciting a strangled scream from him.

"That's an exceptionally mundane point of view," the dead man retorted. "I am far more than a murderer. I am a traveler. From body to body. And a connoisseur of human flesh. Did you know that everyone tastes different?"

"Shut up," Victor growled through clenched teeth, pushing himself backward.

"Rude," the dead man said, sighing, and he kicked Victor in the other thigh.

Victor let out a gasping shriek and collapsed to the floor. His eyes locked onto Ariana for a split second, and he saw her eyelashes flutter as she regained consciousness.

Forcing himself up, Victor snarled at the dead man. "You're an animal. That's it. Nothing more. Damn, you're not even that. You're a parasite."

"I'm a predator!" the ghost hissed, and he punched Victor in the face.

The blow sank into Victor's sinuses, and the pain was excruciating.

Weeping, Victor continued to try for the back wall.

The dead man laughed and shook his head.

"Where on earth do you think you're going?" he asked Victor. "There is no door there. And you don't have the strength to get up and open a window. Do you think that even if you had, I would allow you to escape?"

"Shut up," Victor sobbed, desperately trying to keep the ghost's attention on him.

"No, my rude man," the dead man said, "I will not. In a few moments, I'm going to begin to hurt you. Oh yes, I haven't started anything yet. Then, when I'm done, I'm going to see what I can do with that bonnie little lass of yours. I think she and I might have a bit of fun, especially since I had to sacrifice my last friend just to distract you."

"No," Victor whispered, closing his eyes and shaking his head. "You can't."

"Oh, I can," the dead man said, chuckling. "And I most certainly will."

Victor let out another scream as a cold, biting blow struck him in the stomach.

***

Ariana's head pounded, and Victor's cries of pain cut through her mercilessly. Her heart ached at his suffering, and she hated herself for the sensation it caused.

But as she opened her eyes, she realized he was suffering for a reason.

The man had backed himself into a corner, the ghost's attention fully upon him. And as she watched the ghost torture Victor Daniels, she knew what needed to be done.

Without moving more than a fraction of an inch and forcing herself to ignore the horrific agony Victor was allowing himself to suffer, Ariana located the iron hammer.

It was only inches from her hand.

She reached out, blood soaking into the white cotton glove, and grasped the handle of the hammer.

Victor let out a high pierced shriek, and she didn't let herself look, not even when the dead man laughed, and Victor's voice rose an octave higher.

Instead, she looked at the corpse and saw the silver class ring on the dead woman's finger.

Rising to her knees, Ariana raised the hammer above her head with both hands and brought it smashing down.

Beneath the weapon the ring exploded, a small, contained force that was strong enough to throw her backward, but not nearly enough to destroy the apartment.

For a long time, Ariana lay on her back, staring at the cracked ceiling. Then, with a weary sigh, she rolled over and got to her feet, the hammer still in her hand.

CHAPTER 44:
A LITTLE CHAT

Detective Sara Milton stood inside the hospital room. Victor Daniels was in a medically induced coma. The doctors had no explanation for the severe organ damage he had suffered, but they knew he needed to be under anesthesia for the damage to heal properly.

Elizabeth Crocker entered the room, nodded to Sara and went to check on Victor. After a few moments, she turned around and went back to Sara.

"Detective," the woman said.

Sara raised an eyebrow, hesitated, then said, "Oh, what the hell. Tell me, Ms. Crocker, what happened?"

"I wouldn't know," Elizabeth said. "I received a call from Victor that he had found something. I got there a short time after you did."

"You said all of that with a straight face," Sara said.

Elizabeth nodded. "Of course I did. I'm good at what I do."

"And what exactly do you do, Ms. Crocker?" Sara asked.

"Bad things," the woman replied, and the chill in her voice made Sara understand the woman wasn't joking. "He'll be alright?"

"A couple of days. Maybe more," Sara said. "We got a hold of his son in Pennsylvania, and a brother down in Nashua. A Shane Ryan?"

Elizabeth smiled. "Yes. Good. Will they both be coming up?"

"That's the word I got," Sara said. "Will you be staying around, Ms. Crocker?"

"No," the woman replied.

"Good," Sara stated. "Don't let the door hit you on the way out."

Without another word, Detective Sara Milton left the hospital and went to search for more information on Victor Daniels and Shane Ryan, two brothers with different names.

Betty Crocker, she thought wryly, *is a dead end.*

***

At the far corner of the Odd Fellows Rest Cemetery in New Orleans, a small clump of earth churned. The grass was pulled down, mingling with a curiously dark loom, and bits of debris and dead leaves were caught in the mesmerizing ebb and flow of the ground as night settled onto the city.

The hole widened, deepened, and then a disturbing sucking sound filled the peaceful air of the cemetery.

An old and pale hand punched up through the earth, the bent fingers uncurling to reach towards the night sky. A moment later a second hand joined the first, and both of them grasped the sides of the hole. The thin fingers dug into the sides and within a heartbeat, the aged head of Leanne Le Monde appeared once again beneath the sky of the mortal and mundane world.

She wore the same clothes that she had slipped back into the world below with. Her expression was dour, hate sparkling in her eyes. She clambered out of the ground and sat on the edge of the hole, peering at her surroundings. It took her a short amount of time to realize where she was, but when she did, Leanne nodded with satisfaction.

Where I want to be, she thought, getting gingerly to her feet. *Where I need to be.*

Humming to herself, Leanne brushed the dirt off her clothes and started to limp along the weed-choked paths of the cemetery, searching for the tomb she needed.

***

Stefan Korzh lay in a half daze on his back, staring up at the ceiling with his single eye. At some point in the evening, he had fallen asleep, almost for two hours before the alarm near the main gate had gone off.

A review of the footage had shown a fox as it slipped back into the shadows.

Sleep would find him again soon, and until it did, Stefan would lay on his back and wait for it. He repeated the process every night, from seven in the evening until seven in the morning, and only once the sun was fully out and illuminated the land, did he risk any ventures outside of his armed camp.

Anne Le Morte's caretaker had fired at him 39 more times since the first occasion. At all hours of the day and night, whenever he dared to make an appearance, Stefan could expect a gunshot. The caretaker had an uncanny knack of firing off a round just as he was drifting off to sleep.

And I'm not sure where they even are, he thought morosely.

He had found where they had been, but always at least a day behind.

The woods were undeniably Anne's territory, and she knew it better than he could with his time curtailed and limited to daylight. Stefan knew that if he ventured into the woods after dark, the night-vision goggles he owned would be useless once the dead woman drained the batteries of power.

He would be at her mercy and the thought of it was as repulsive as it was frightening.

How long? he asked himself. *I can't stay here and hide. I did that with Ariana and my father. I almost allowed their hunter to do me in.*

I can't let Anne Le Morte control my actions any longer. I will speak to father, Stefan thought, nodding. *Perhaps I can get him to call her off, and once that is done, get rid of him before he can unleash her again.*

The idea pleased him, and Stefan closed his eyes.

I still have to get away, he reminded himself as exhaustion overwhelmed him.

They're both still out there.

But Stefan smiled.

He had gotten away from them before, and he would do so again.

* * *

Concord, NH
January 6th, 1999

Patrolwoman Sara Milton stamped her feet and muttered under her breath. Her shift had started half an hour earlier, and it was already a miserable night.

She stood outside of her cruiser, parked on the bridge over the Turkey River on Iron Works Road. A pair of inmates had escaped from the State Prison's halfway house, and now she and most of the third shift were scattered around the Russell-Shea State Forest, making sure the inmates didn't get away.

Stupid, Sara grumbled. *Who in the hell runs away on a night like this?*

Stupid!

She tilted her head back, exhaled angrily and watched the clouds of her own breath curl up into the night sky. Originally, the forecast had called for a snowstorm, but it was too cold for any new snow to fall.

A loud, sharp crack rang out through the bitter cold, and her head jerked down fast enough to catch a glimpse of a white face vanishing back into the tree line.

Sara snatched her radio off her hip and spoke into it.

"I've got a possible inmate," she said. "Iron Works Road, bridge."

"Copy," the dispatcher said.

Within minutes, a pair of cruisers raced up to her, and Sergeants Dan Stevens and Brian Rocco got out of their vehicles. They took flashlights and shotguns out.

"Staying warm, Milton?" Sergeant Stevens asked, smiling at her.

"Not enough, Sergeant," she answered.

"Maybe," Sergeant Rocco began, but he was cut off by a high, terrified shriek.

Both of the men swore and took off running towards the edge of the bridge, sliding down through the snow that covered the embankment and staying away from the river. They slogged their way into the forest, and vanished, the bobbing of their flashlights marking their passage.

Sara knew she had to remain by the cars, and she was furious about it. She drew her pistol and called in the situation. Sergeant Rocco's voice came over the radio a moment later, detailing the pursuit, and the fact that there were three subjects they were in pursuit of, not two.

Seconds later, one of the sergeants fired a shotgun. Then the sounds of the weapons being fired overlapped and filled the night.

The sounds of engines revving swallowed the last notes of the weapons, and as headlights appeared around the curves, Sara hurried to the edge of the bridge. Her eyes scanned the tree line, her weapon up.

A heartbeat later, a man raced out of the trees and screamed at her.

The man, tall and nearly as thin as the saplings around him, wore a hospital gown and nothing more. His head was covered in bald patches and short, bright red hair. His hands looked too large for his arms.

He opened his mouth impossibly wide, and let out another scream, one that turned into a shriek and shook her to her core.

The first of the reinforcements arrived, and the headlights on the cruiser punched through the tall man with the ease of a flashlight through wax-paper.

As the cruiser's brakes squealed, the tall man vanished.

The officer behind the wheel jumped out, hurried to her side and asked in a low, confused voice, "What the hell was that?"

"I don't know," Sara whispered, hating the way her pistol shook in her hand. "God help me, I don't know."

CONFUSED AND ANGRY

Neither Dan Stevens nor Brian Rocco had survived the encounter in the woods.

And no one who wasn't specifically given permission by the chief of Concord PD was allowed to look at the crime scene. Even the Police Union had told everyone to back off.

Sara sat in a small interrogation room with a captain from the State Police, the Police Union's attorney Don MacMillan, and no recording equipment whatsoever.

She wasn't being questioned, but she felt like a prisoner.

The captain, a tall, heavily built man who hadn't given her his name, tapped the battered tabletop with a Bic pen. He had jotted down half a page of notes on a yellow legal pad, but that was all.

Finally, the man sighed and said, "You can't talk about this."

"What?" Sara asked, glancing at Don.

The attorney shook his head.

"You're serious," Sara said, feeling her anger rise. "We've got two cops dead, and you don't want me talking about this? To anyone, or just the press?"

"You can't talk about this to anyone, Officer Milton," the captain said, a look of distaste on his face as he spoke. "If you're Catholic, and you go to confession, you can't even tell your father confessor. Do you understand?"

Sara flashed a glare at Don.

But before he spoke, the captain snapped, "Officer!"

She jerked in her seat and looked back at him.

He put the pen down on the table, closed his eyes and pinched the bridge of his nose. The captain then took a deep breath, lowered his hand and opened his eyes.

"Do not think," he said in a slow, calm voice, "that any of us are pleased with this situation. Or that this directive comes from me. Far from it. I have my orders. You have your orders. Don't speak to anyone. Not a soul about this. Do you understand me?"

She saw the real anger and pain on his face, and she swallowed her own and nodded.

"Thank you," the captain said, sighing. He stood up, looked at them and said, "Don, officer, thank you. It's not easy. And it won't be. But we'll leave it where it needs to be right now."

The captain took his pen and legal pad with him when he left.

"Sara," Don said, "keep cool, alright?"

"What are they going to do?" she demanded.

"Fire you." The statement was made in such a simple, plain way that it took her a moment to process what the attorney had said.

"Really?" she asked, stunned.

Don nodded. "They've made it clear. Anyone who speaks, well, they'll get rid of them. And you'll never work in law enforcement again. Whatever happened out there, they want to keep a lid on it."

"Don, I don't even know what happened out there!" she shouted.

He held up his hands. "Easy, easy, Sara. I know that. Everyone knows that. The thing is, you were the closest one to the scene. You're the only one who saw whoever it was that killed them."

"How hard can it be to find him?" Sara asked. "There's a foot of snow on the ground out there, and I swear that guy was just about naked."

"I don't have any answers," Don said. "Listen, Sara, for your own sake, don't say anything. Alright?"

She gave a short, angry nod, and then stormed out of the room, furious with the world.

EXPLORATION

After two weeks of silence, and pretending nothing had happened, Sara made her way to the scene.

She and some of her colleagues were frustrated by the fact that the two inmates who had started the entire episode were still at large.

And they weren't listed as possible murder suspects of the sergeants. In fact, the deaths of the two men were listed as mutilation by a rabid animal of some sort. There was one theory that if it was an animal it might possibly be a mountain lion. The only issue was that the State itself denied that mountain lions were even in New Hampshire.

This is absurd, Sara said, parking her jeep just off the road and climbing out of it. *No one can keep their stories straight, and we aren't even allowed to talk about who might have killed them.*

She pulled the hood of her coat up, secured the strap beneath her chin and walked down the embankment. For nearly five minutes, Sara followed the path that had been worn through the snow by the various forensics teams that had gone into the forest. When she reached the scene, she stopped and snorted in disgust.

The place had been scrubbed clean by the forensics teams, and nothing was left that might have served as a clue towards who had murdered the two sergeants.

She grimaced, then started to search the small area. Sara found evidence of the shotgun blasts, but the teams had dug the slugs out of the trees. Sinking down into a squat, she peered around, trying to decide which way the killers could have come from, or fled towards.

A pale piece of wood caught her eye, and she moved forward.

Reaching out, Sara took hold of a small, broken branch. Only a fraction of the pale wood was visible, but it was enough.

Standing up, Sara moved several feet deeper into the forest and dropped down again. She let her eyes relax, and in a few moments, she spotted another piece of evidence. A torn bit of bark laying on the snow.

Sara followed the faint, almost negligible trail. Her back ached as did her legs, and she kept glancing back to make certain she was leaving enough of her own trail to follow back.

Satisfied, she continued on. Her heart beat quicker, her blood racing through her veins. She knew the killers were near.

Sara could feel it, a dull, heavy certainty in her stomach that spiked her brain with adrenaline and caused her breath to rush in and out.

They're up ahead, she thought, pausing to take her pistol out. *I'm coming for you.*

The faint odor of a campfire reached her nose, and she picked up her pace, her excitement spurring her forward.

She almost stumbled into a small glade, bringing her pistol up and leveling it on the first figure she saw. Her shout of joy died in her throat when she looked at the scene in front of her and realized that the men were indeed there, but she wasn't sure if all of them were there.

She identified two heads, three arms, and at least three hands. Too many intestines hung from the tree limbs, and she found herself wondering if she was standing in any part of the men.

When she glanced down, something struck her from behind that sent her sprawling forward.

Landing in a pile of legs and feet, Sara let out a furious howl and twisted around onto her back, bringing her pistol up.

The same, tall, thin man she had seen the night the sergeants had died stood in front of her.

He shrieked, and Sara put six rounds into the center of his chest.

But nothing happened.

Not a single, red blossom formed on his pale, light blue hospital gown.

Instead, he hurled himself forward, and as he leapt toward her, a loud blast filled her ears, and the man vanished.

"Well," a cold, slight voice said from behind her, "you're quick, I'll give you that."

Sara got to her feet and looked at the man who had spoken.

An older black man stood beside the remains of the inmates' campfire, smoking a ridiculously large pipe. It reached from his mouth to almost the center of his chest in a long 'J' with smoke curling up out of vents in the silver cap over the bowl.

In his yellow-gloved hands he held a sawed-off shotgun, and on his head, he had what she could only identify as an Elmer Fudd hunting hat. He wore an equally absurd looking plaid coat that was easily as old as she was. His pants were a thick, blue corduroy tucked into tall, Wellington engineer's boots.

"Who are you?" she demanded.

"You can call me King," he answered.

"Is that your name?" she asked.

He nodded. "King Kincaid. Now, come along, Officer Milton, it's getting colder out, and Angelo won't stay away for long."

"Wait. What?" Sara asked. "How do you know my name? And who are you talking about?"

King took a long draw off his pipe, exhaled through his nose and said, "First, you were identified as one who may take it upon themselves to dig a little deeper. Since there was only one female listed, I assumed you were she. Second, I am speaking of Angelo Frattelone. The dead man who killed two of Concord's finest, and these two less than estimable men. So, now that I've answered your questions, let's get out of here. I'm cold. I need to go to the bathroom. And I'd like to be somewhere a little warmer when Angelo reappears."

Confused, Sara followed the small man out of the glade and wondered what to do about the remains of the men in the trees behind her.

IN THE HOME OF KING KINCAID

King's home was a small camper in the bed of a battered, dark blue pick-up truck of indeterminate age and origin. The vehicle was parked across from the State Hospital's cemetery, and the tight confines of the camper were surprisingly comfortable.

Both Sara and King had shed their outer layers, hanging them up on dull brass hooks set in the back of the camper door. They sat at a small table, and a portable electric heater put out a surprising amount of warmth.

King had traded his long pipe for a much shorter one, and while the tobacco in the bowl was unlit, he kept the stem of it clamped between his teeth. He had made some instant coffee when they first escaped from the bite of the January chill, and he had seasoned the brew liberally with apple brandy.

The older man leaned back against his seat, smiled around the pipe, and asked, "How's the coffee, officer?"

"Good," Sara confessed. She had never been a fan of instant anything, but the mixture of alcohol and caffeine worked wonders against the chill that had settled in her bones.

"Glad to hear it," he said. King removed a box of matches from the table, extracted a wooden match and struck it. Soon, he had his pipe lit and a sweet smell that reminded Sara of the brandy filled the air. The smoke curled up from the bowl, hung lazily about the man's head for a moment, then dispersed into the camper to vanish among the nooks and crannies, settling in and adding a layer to the powerful sense of comfort the camper exuded.

For several minutes, Sara drank her coffee in silence, wanting to ask King a slew of questions, but managing to keep them to herself. He had a small smile on his face as he enjoyed his pipe.

When she decided it was time to speak, King beat her to it.

"I imagine you've held your tongue long enough," he said, straightening up.

"I have," she replied.

"Alright, would you ask me a question, or would you rather I speak?" He raised his eyebrows inquisitively and waited.

Sara cleared her throat, then said, "Speak. Please."

He gave her a nod of acquiescence.

"As you know, my name is King Kincaid," the man said, "and I told you about the danger of Angelo. You, in turn, seem to disbelieve your own eyes."

She scoffed. "How can I believe them? I saw a man vanish into thin air. Something's going on. I know there was some talk a few years ago about the possibility of illegal dumping in the Turkey River."

"And you think the answer to what you saw is a smattering of heavy metals or toxic dyes?" King asked, chuckling. "You're not stupid, officer, anyone can see that. Don't limit yourself."

She bristled at the statement, but she bit her tongue and waited for the man to continue.

"Back in 1943, when I was only a few years younger than you are now," King said, "I had the pleasure of meeting a great man. His name was John Steinbeck, and he was writing about the war. He was in Europe, traveling to different airfields to speak with the crews and the ground teams for the bombers. I was on one of the teams. Nothing more than an armorer, really, and lucky to be there. Now, Mr. Steinbeck spoke to me like I was a man, and if you know anything about the 1940s, officer, you know that wasn't exactly the norm."

Sara nodded.

"Good." King was silent a moment before he spoke again. "When Mr. Steinbeck was there, I didn't believe in ghosts or gremlins or goblins. But both he and I were newly arrived, and by the time he left, we both believed. We had borne witness to ghosts wandering the airfields. Dead men who hadn't quite realized they were dead. Goblins found killed in the bombings of German positions. Hell, you should have seen the state of some of the bombers that came back. The damage that was done wasn't from any anti-aircraft weapons. No, plain old gremlins. Nasty little creatures that climb into engines and tear them to bits."

King sighed and shook his head. "Well, the point of this is, my eyes were opened up, and when I got home from the war and went back to Springfield, Massachusetts, I did a little more digging. And the more digging I did, the more truth came out. You know how it is, I suspect."

"I do," Sara said, wondering where the man's rambling speech was going.

"Thought so. And I think you would like to know what the point is that I'm driving at," King said with a wink. "The point, officer, is that I discovered the dead don't all rest. Not in the least. There are more than a few that seem to take it upon themselves to cause some sort of misery and mischief. With that realization, I started to hunt them."

Sara frowned, then asked him, "Are you telling me that ghosts are real?"

"What do you think?" King asked, his voice becoming hard. "What did you see out there?"

"I saw two corpses and a figure that disappeared," she answered. "And even if ghosts are real, which I'm not saying they are, they can't hurt people. They would just be, I don't know, ghosts."

"Look out the window," King said in a low voice, "and tell me what you see."

Sara turned partially in the seat and did as the old man said.

What she saw was the cemetery, most of the gravestones hidden by the deep snow of mid-January.

"Nothing," she answered, facing him again. "Why, what do you see?"

"I see the dead," King said, relighting his pipe. He shook out the match and dropped it into the brass ashtray on the Formica tabletop. "Granted, there aren't many of them out there. But I see them. To the right, about twenty feet from the center, there's a young woman. By the crook of her neck, I figure she hung herself. Beyond her, and back a bit, there's an older lady. From what I can see, she had cataracts when she died. Poor thing was probably as blind as a bat."

Sara felt uncomfortable as the man spoke, his voice slow and smooth as he described three more people. She wanted to tell him he had an active imagination, but she knew that wasn't the case.

"How do you know that?" she asked, her words spoken in a husky tone.

"I can see them," King replied, "as easily and as clearly as I can see you sitting here with me."

Sara must have made a face because the old man smiled, a chuckle escaping his lips. He drew in on the pipe, exhaled, and then continued.

"The talent isn't common, but it's not exactly rare either," he stated. "Most of us are born with some amount of it. Children are especially attune to their natural abilities. Yet as they grow older, those abilities, if not nurtured, whither, and die upon the vine. I had let mine whither, and it wasn't until I had spent my time overseas that it came back to me. Sitting around a fire with Mr. Steinbeck, waiting for our bombers to come home and watching the dead make themselves known, well, that heightened my ability, I can tell you that."

King paused before he added, "I didn't want to lose that ability again. Or to forget what I saw during the war. So, I continued to look for them when I came home."

Sara risked a glance out the window to make certain she still couldn't see anything, then said, "What do you do when you see them?"

"Mostly, I don't do much," King answered. "You see all sorts of nonsense about guiding people to the light. Only a few want to, did you know that?"

She shook her head.

"It's true. Most of the dead who hang around afterward, well, they're downright happy to do so," he said with a snort. "Some of them, like the ones in the graveyard, they're confused. Not sure if they're coming or going. The monks called me in, asked me to speak with the dead. They hadn't realized there were quite so many here."

"Hold on?" Sara said, lifting a hand to stop him. "What monks are you talking about?"

"The Benedictines at St. Anselm College in Manchester," King said. "Are there others in the area?"

"No," Sara said. "Why would they call you? Why would they know anything about it?"

"The world is a lot stranger than you think, officer," King said in a gentle voice. "And there is a great deal going on in it that no one truly knows about."

"Guess so," she muttered and finished her coffee.

"Now, with all of that being said," the old man continued, "what are you planning on doing about Angelo?"

Surprised, Sara asked, "What do you mean?"

"Officer," King said, his voice becoming hard, "that dead man killed two of your colleagues. I'm fairly certain it's time for him to go away for good."

Sara nodded, looked down at the mug in her hands, and asked, "And how do we do that, Mr. Kincaid?"

"Carefully," the old man said with a dry chuckle, and let the smoke from his pipe curl out of the corners of his mouth.

Peaslee Annex Wing, State Hospital

Sara was tired and more nervous than she cared to admit.

She stood beside King Kincaid and could find no warmth in the sunshine that pierced the dull gray clouds of the early morning sky.

"You okay?" King asked, checking his shotgun.

"It's Saturday morning," Sara said bitterly, "and I'm standing outside an abandoned piece of state property that I'm about to break into."

"*We're* about to break into," King corrected.

"You want to tell me why again?" she asked, shifting the stiff bag she was holding from her left hand to her right.

King chuckled at her nervousness and said, "Inside the building is a small, wooden cross. It belonged to Angelo. He's bound himself to it. As long as that cross is left lying about, he'll be able to get around."

"How do you know that?" Sara said, asking the question she had told herself she wouldn't. "How can you?"

"The dead can speak," King said softly. "Some of them can be quite helpful. There was one such nearby. A young girl killed in a car accident across from the hospital. She told me all about Angelo."

King sighed and smiled at Sara. "We need to find it, put it in the bag you're holding, and call it a day."

"This bag?" she asked, holding it up to inspect it again. "What's so special about a burlap sack?"

"Lead and iron filaments are woven through it," King said, "and a fair amount of salt has been spread around as well."

"And those things will stop the ghost?" she asked, hating herself for saying the word.

"They will," King said. "Alright. We should get this done. I imagine the electricity is off in the building, so we need to find that cross before we lose the daylight."

Sara found the idea of being in the decrepit old asylum after nightfall repulsive, and she repressed a shudder of revulsion.

King saw it and nodded.

"Remember," he said, taking the lead, "don't get in front of me when I have a shot."

"Don't worry," Sara said. "I have no desire to be hit with a load of buckshot."

King let out his dry chuckle. "Lord no, this isn't loaded with buckshot. I've got rock-salt rounds. Cheaper to make, and just as effective. Painful though. Terribly so."

They advanced on the tall, four-story brick building with quick steps, and Sara tried not to think about what she had read about the place.

"Do you know about this building?" King asked.

Sara groaned and said, "Yes."

"Good," the man replied. "It's important to keep it in mind. The men housed here were dangerous, which is why Angelo's ghost is never far from it. He was judged criminally insane and died here. What you need to remember, officer, is that he wasn't the only one to have passed away in the building. Many others did as well, and more than a few never had their bodies claimed by their relatives. This means there is a distinct possibility that we will encounter another ghost."

"Let's just stop with the whole 'ghost' word, okay?" Sara said, uncomfortable with her rising fear. "We're hunting something. That's all. Just something."

"Don't let the word get the better of you," King said in a tone that brokered no disagreement. "Call it by what it is, and it won't have power over you."

Sara grumbled, but she didn't disagree.

The man was right.

Focusing on the building ahead of them, she refused to let her fears advance any further.

Soon they stood at a pair of temporary gates made out of chain-link fence. King took out a pair of wire cutters and opened a hole in the left gate.

This is terrible, Sara thought, following King into the snow-covered parking lot. Their footsteps were loud, echoing off the walls of the building as they drew closer, the old man on an arrow-straight course for a door covered in plywood.

Using the wire cutters, King cut the heads off several exposed nails and pulled the wood aside. The remaining nails screamed as steel dragged against the frame, and a moment later a gaping doorway stood before them.

King glanced over his shoulder at her and asked, "Are you ready?"

Sara's throat clenched, and all she could do was nod.

The old man produced a flashlight from a pocket and turned it on, the bright beam cutting through the darkness beyond.

When they stepped into the building, Sara noticed the bitter cold and the smell of rot and damp. Scents that should not have existed in the harsh January temperatures.

Why is it colder in here than outside? she asked herself, repressing a shiver.

King stepped lightly around broken beer bottles and crushed cans. A few tattered blankets were piled in one corner of a room that looked as though it had been a custodian's office at one time. The door across from them was open, hanging weakly from the lower hinge.

"Now," King said in a soft voice, "there's going to be a closet in the hallway up ahead. In it, we'll find Angelo's cross. I'll pick it up and put it into the bag. You just keep that bag closed. We won't have any problem with him if you do that."

"What happens if I don't?" Sara asked.

"Then he gets out," King replied dryly, "and I doubt he'll be happy about it."

The light of the old man's flashlight played across the peeling paint of the hallway's walls and stopped at a closed door. Like its surroundings, the door was battered and worn and affected the primal part of Sara that demanded she run from the building.

She fought back the urge to do just that and tried to understand why such a banal part of life should cause her to be afraid.

And she couldn't.

A snarl behind them caused her to jerk around.

Angelo Frattelone stood in the janitor's room, weaving back and forth on his feet. His lip was curled up into a sneer, and he spoke in a mixture of Italian and gibberish.

"A wooden cross," King said calmly, handing her his flashlight and bringing the shotgun up to his shoulder. "Find it, now, officer."

Angelo leaped towards them, and the shotgun roared.

Sara's head instantly began to ache, the blood pounding in her ringing ears. Swearing, she tore the closet door open and peered inside. Dimly, she heard the old man reload the weapon, the spent casing clattering on the floor. She stepped into the room and looked at filthy shelves covered in a layer of dust.

But they were empty, barren of anything except the dust and dried mouse droppings.

She jumped when Angelo screamed in front of her, and the shotgun went off again, rock salt tearing into the walls.

Embarrassed, she crouched down and searched under the bottom shelves, and directly in front of her she saw the cross.

It was a worn, gnawed upon piece of wood, and when she pulled it out from beneath the shelf, she saw that human teeth had marked it. The cross was painfully cold, even through the gloves she wore, and she lifted it up for a closer look.

"The bag, girl!" King snapped, startling her into obedience.

As she dropped the cross into the confines of the bag and cinched it closed, she heard a step behind her.

She risked a glance as she stood and saw King's grim visage. He held out his hand, and sheepishly she handed it to him.

He nodded his thanks, tugged the bag into one of the large pockets of his jacket, and motioned for her to follow.

They moved at a faster pace out of the building, the old man almost jogging.

When they reached the parking lot, Sara took in a deep breath and shuddered, the adrenaline dumping out of her system and into her stomach.

She stopped, but King only hesitated to gently take her by the arm and urge her forward again.

Soon, they had slipped through the fence and were back in his camper. He mixed the same instant coffee and apple brandy for both of them and placed the bag with the cross within in an old, iron safe.

"What will you do with it?" Sara asked.

"I've a friend I need to speak with," King replied. "He doesn't advocate the destruction of possessed items. He serves as a warden of sorts, keeping the items and their residents within a secure building. Should I give Angelo to him, the dead man will be kept away for the safety of others."

"Why don't you destroy the cross?" Sara said. "Will that set him free?"

"In a manner of speaking," the old man replied. "He will be obliterated. Nothing will remain of his soul. I don't know if I feel comfortable doing that. The man was mad when he was alive, and mad he still is. Should he be destroyed for an illness?"

Sara hesitated, then said, "I can't make that decision."

"Neither can I," King responded, and silence settled over the camper.

* * *

Check out these best-selling series from our talented authors:

GHOST STORIES

RON RIPLEY

BERKLEY STREET SERIES
MOVING IN SERIES
HAUNTED COLLECTION SERIES
DEATH HUNTER SERIES

IAN FORTEY

JIGSAW OF SOULS SERIES
CULT OF THE ENDLESS NIGHT SERIES

SUPERNATURAL SUSPENSE

A. I. NASSER

SLAUGHTER SERIES
SIN SERIES

DAVID LONGHORN

NIGHTMARE SERIES
ASYLUM SERIES

SARA CLANCY

THE BELL WITCH SERIES
BANSHEE SERIES

For a complete list of our new releases and best-selling horror books, visit ScareStreet.com or scan the QR code below!